The Autobiography of
Francis N. Stein:
The Last Promethean

The Autobiography of Francis N. Stein: The Last Promethean

A. ROONEY

MADVILLE
PUBLISHING

Lake Dallas, Texas

Printed in the United States of America

FIRST EDITION
Requests for permission to reproduce material from this work should be sent to:

     Permissions
     Madville Publishing LLC
     P.O. Box 358
     Lake Dallas, TX 75065

Cover Design by Jacqueline Davis
Author Photograph by Kalika Mehta

ISBN: 978-1-948692-08-3 paperback, and 978-1-948692-09-0 ebook
Library of Congress Control Number: 2018960111

To the Frankensteins of this world.
Hang in there, brothers.
A part of you is in each of us.

Part 1

Chapter 1

Robeson was saying something about all they needed to do was get the big tarp over the truck and "ain't nobody gonna know it's here. Don't drive it, though, if you want to avoid gettin' busted."

When they'd gotten the bungees attached, he said, "Where you been, Francis? We ain't seen you for months, man."

Francis wanted to tell him a much bigger story, of bears and beating hearts and fires, but instead said he'd been working on a ranch, out near Doveless, for someone named Pindar.

"They been lookin' for you," Robeson said.

Who's been looking? Francis asked.

"The hound been lookin' everywhere for you, man, the detectives. They think you had somethin' to do with killin' that dude at the club. Even though Hennie and all the girls said, no, no, we didn't see him that night, no, he wasn't workin'."

Francis asked if Hennie had said anything else, that it was her car the thief was after. That he'd been coming around and he was in the parking lot that night trying to get into her car. And that he was smoking marijuana and calling out things to him.

"'A big dude,' the cops said, 'marks all over his head and

arms,' they said. Big dude, we said. 'Yeah, yeah,' they said. With lotta marks on his head, we said. 'Yeah, yeah,' they said. Never heard of him, we said. We told 'em we didn't know nothin' about you. You got to watch, Francis. Them hard-ass cops gonna pick you up, beat you on the head, and then your brains gonna be gone forever."

Francis looked around at Robeson and the city and was surprised to find himself there again. He put his hand on the still warm hood and when they finished with the truck, Francis asked if there was some place he could stay, somebody he could stay with.

"I leased this big basement from the furniture store upstairs. They had it for rent. Three hundred bucks, if you can believe it, clean too. People been livin' with me, but we could use one more. You got a fart sack or anything? And if you can help out a little bit with the rent."

Francis asked about blankets and sheets, a pillow or two, he didn't have a sleeping bag, and Robeson said he could loan him some bedding until he got on his feet.

I got nothing right now for sleeping, but I could help out on the rent. And then if I get a job, I'll help out a little more, return your stuff.

"What was you doin' on that ranch, man? I didn't know you knew how to be a cowboy. I see you got a nice new scar on your head too."

Francis said they used pick-ups mostly to herd the cows and he stayed in a bunkhouse. He held back explaining about the organ transplants. Somedays it was pretty hard work, he said, but he liked it. And the scar came when he jumped off the train and hit his head.

"If you liked it so much, how come you're here, man? What happened? I know somethin' must have happened, troublesome cat that you are. You didn't kill one of those other motherfuckin' cowboys did you?"

2

Francis said that he never meant to; he didn't feel like he had a choice.

"Goddamn it, Francis. You are gonna bring the fuckin' pigs down on us, man."

He came looking for me in the old west town, Francis said. He had his gun out and was going to shoot me. What could I do?

"If they come lookin' for you, man, you got to get outta here. Know what I'm sayin'? You'll fuck it up for the rest of us, and they'll find reasons to pick us up too."

He shot the coyote, so I knew he had a gun.

"What the hell you talkin' about, man? Old west town, coyote. You musta bumped your head more than once out there?"

And then there was Pindar.

"Pindar is who? The dude in the old west town?"

Francis told Robeson that Pindar was the person who owned the ranch and that he brought in people to forcefully take his blood and then his heart. That's why he left.

"I got no idea what you just said. You weren't this goofy when you left, man. You better pay up your part of the rent today, Francis. You ain't gonna be here long."

When I left, Francis said, I set the operating room on fire while Pindar was getting ready. I set it on fire with him inside.

"Pindar in the operating room? I thought you was on a ranch? Better get you a bottle full of aspirin."

It was a regular ranch that did organ transplants, mostly for rich people. Hard to believe, now that I think about it. And Pindar was the owner. He tried to take my blood. He took my blood and then he was going to take my heart.

"Dude, this bullshit is beyond strange. Your blood and your heart. Like some kind of weird vampire-werewolf thing. You must have a special kind of heart."

3

Who is staying here Robeson? Who's here?

"Madam Pham and the Twins, and Alferd Packer the eighth, but we hardly ever see him. Once in a while Cross. And everybody's got their own room."

What is Cross now; how's he dressing?

"He's dressin' like a tennis queen, white skirt and all."

You got a toilet down here, Robeson? I need to use the toilet.

Which room you want me in? Francis asked. He said that he'd been up all night and needed a nap. He'd driven the truck on the back roads from the ranch to Denver and it took forever.

"The bathroom is by the door, Francis. There's a room with a bed and mattress and a chest of drawers. But that bed's gonna be way too small for you. Oh, and I forgot to tell you. There's a dude that comes around, Chancellor, we call him Chan. He stays with the Twins sometimes. He's in charge of the college and he comes late at night after his meetings. Don't nobody s'posed to know he stays with us, visits. But don't seem like nobody cares."

Any kind of work I could do. Anybody got anything going on?

"We got a gig comin' up."

What kind of gig?

"Alferd's been workin at the RTD as some kind of official transit rider, but there's another part. He sets it up so that if you're on a designated bus, one of the smaller routes, then that bus has like a little accident and everybody gets hurt, but nobody seriously. All you got to do is fall down when the driver steps on the brakes to avoid, like, somebody at the curb and hold your knee or your neck."

And RTD doesn't know what's going on? They don't know people are faking?

"It's one of the big bosses. An insurance scam. He gets a kick and he spreads it around."

4

How long before they give you money?

"They make you wait at the bus until the legal dude comes. Then they do a quick evaluation and the next day you get a check, to cover the chiropractor or drugs, whatever. The big boss somehow gets part of your money."

How much people been getting?

"A couple thou. If you're a good actor, maybe three on top of that."

And that's it, no more, or more later?

"Another check comes whether you need it or not. And if you can get Dr. Crack-a-Back to submit the bill for more, you can split it with him."

How many have you done? How many times have you gotten money?

"Just once, but everybody else has done it a bunch of times."

Any place to get something cheap to eat?

"Madame Pham's still owning a noodle place, Pho 36, a new place. She sold the other one on Federal Boulevard. If you do something for her in the back, she'll give you a bowl of noodles, pot of tea. And she's there now till midnight or later. We're kinda together, me and Madam."

How do I get there? I've only been to the old place.

"Take the 15 to Peoria and it's in the shopette near where you get off, south side of the street."

Where you going now?

"Work. I've been helpin' this dude with his roach coach for dinner. I'm gonna give you a key so you can come and go. If you come in late try not to make noise. I'll get an extra pillow and blanket off my bed."

I appreciate it, Robeson. I'll try to stay out of trouble.

"And Francis. . . ."

What?

"Don't say nothin' if the Chancellor is here drinkin' wine with the Twins. He might want to talk, so just talk to him."

All right, Robeson, thanks, man.

"It ain't nothin', 'cept if them pigs show up."

2.

The bus driver asked Francis "You a senior, big fella? A dollar and ten cents is strictly seniors. If you ain't a senior, it's two-twenty. To be honest, you don't look like no senior. You got to show me some I.D. or you're gonna have to put another dollar and a dime in the fare box."

Francis said, All I have is a thousand-dollar bill. I don't have anything else.

"If you got a thousand-dollar bill, you shouldn't be on this bus, big fella. And if you really got a thousand bucks, you better watch yourself. Go ahead and find a seat."

To a woman already seated Francis said, Excuse me, ma'am, do you mind if I sit next to you?

"Long as you keep your hands to yourself," she said. "And you don't take up too much space. And you don't cough or sneeze. And you don't eat your lunch and get it all over."

To a man across the aisle Francis said, Mind if I sit down next to you, sir?

"I don't mind," he said, "but it'll cost you."

Yeah? How much?

"Tall as you are and as much room as you gonna take up, maybe a thousand bucks."

Francis said the next time he got on the bus he'd catch up with him.

"My stop's comin' up, asshole. I'd prefer to have the thousand now."

Francis winced when the man called him an asshole and

said he must have overheard him telling the bus driver about the thousand.

But I was only making that up, Francis said. I didn't have enough money, just some pocket change. I wouldn't know what to do with a thousand dollars.

"Anybody ever tell you you're an ugly son of a bitch."

No, I don't recall anyone ever saying that. You're the first, maybe the last.

"That a threat?" the man asked. "Just cause you're big, that don't scare me. Get off the bus the same time and we'll see."

Francis looked around at the people on the bus, the ads on the walls, the busy street, and the man sitting next to him grinning with eyes wide-open.

I'm too hungry to get off the bus and deal with you. I'm going to Madam's to get something to eat.

"Shit on Madam's head and shit on your ugly head too."

Francis apologized when the man squeezed past him and fell in the aisle. The rear door opened and Francis shoved him and his grocery bags down the stairs and he spilled out onto the curb, face first. A couple took their seats.

"Sir, you can't hold the back door open like that," the driver said. "We have to go. Stay on the bus or get off, and don't cause no ruckus again or I'll buzz the police. Understand?"

Yes, Francis said, sorry. It's just that he . . . , when I sat down, he called me. . . .

"Whatever happened is between you two, understand? We can't have that sort of thing, pushing and fighting, on a public bus. That's your first and last warning. You with me?"

Francis stood and said, Sorry, driver. Won't happen again.

He hadn't ridden the 15 for a few months but it was probably the same as it always was. To no one in particular Francis mumbled Been out in the country, on a ranch, with Pindar. Who might be dead now because of the fire, and his heart.

The bus was full again and a young woman said, "You're welcome to sit here, I'm getting off in two stops."

To the woman Francis said, Thank you and asked if she happened to know which stop was Peoria. He told her he couldn't remember and wondered if they'd missed it.

"Next one after mine. Where you headed?"

Madam Pham's, a Vietnamese noodle place on Peoria.

"It's right there to the right when you get off. Big sign. Tenderloin noodle bowl, number 63, it's the best."

Francis thanked her and said some time if she wanted to eat noodles, that he would . . . and she said she appreciated it but that she was doing only low-carbs.

Next street after this one, Francis reminded himself, is the O street, Oswego, then Peoria.

All right, driver, Francis said waving, sorry about that, sorry about any trouble.

He wondered if Madam would remember him, that he'd met her only a couple times at the Federal place. And maybe once at her house with the Twins. Around the rear and through the kitchen.

"Who is this big one coming to the back now," Madam said, "this tall one. I think you been gone now, yes? Maybe six months. You come to the other place sometimes, ah, with the Twins? Where you been? I hear about you didn't I?"

I've been working, Madam. I've been on a ranch, which also did . . . and today I came back to Denver. What did you hear about me?

"I think maybe you win the lottery. Plenty money, big money, and you want my help to find pretty Vietnamese girl, ah. Maybe buy restaurant from Madam Pham, go Vietnam one day with pretty wife, ah, Big One."

I didn't win the lottery, Madam; no lottery, sorry about that. But if possible I could. . . .

"If possible today you want noodles because you don't have money, ah, and no job? Robeson tell you to come? That guy. Ok, maybe you stay back here with noodles, ah, and then I tell you what I hear. After that you carry rice bags from back and I show you where."

Thank you, Madam, Francis said. I'll carry the bags now if you want. I'll carry the bags before I eat. Where do you want them?

"Food closet. You ok eat pork? You Stein, yeah, no problem? Today we have too much pork and I give you bowl of pork noodles, that ok, and a few neck bones?"

Pork is ok, pork is good.

"Or maybe you don't like pork and you want tenderloin, ah? Sorry only pork today."

When she had a few minutes, Madam told him about the parking lot and the club. That the girls had come in late after work and talked about it. And that the detectives had asked questions when they came to eat.

"The police say if you come, ah, I should call," Madam said. "They said they just want to talk. Ask you about this bad guy in the parking lot. They say he was not a good guy, maybe steal things from cars, houses, all over. And they have video pictures of him. But not you, no pictures. They ask if you tall. I say I can't remember. Maybe tall, maybe short. Just come to restaurant one time."

What have the Twins been doing? Francis asked. Are they working? They got jobs someplace?

"They modeling, ah. Make good money. They meet Chancellor there."

What kind of modeling? Like for clothes, fashion, that sort of thing?

"Different kind of modeling."

Any other kind of work you got? Anything else you want me to do? I have time tonight.

9

"No, I see you later with Robeson in basement, at furniture store. How you going home?"

I'll go back the same way. Hop on the 15. Maybe get off and have a beer, walk the rest of the way.

"Be careful. Lots of police on Colfax. And you too big to hide, ah. You want to take pork noodles home?"

No, thank you, Madam. That was plenty. I like the pork noodles here. And I can do more work, I can work for you again.

"Maybe take noodles for Robeson."

Yeah, ok, I'll take some for Robeson. Is he just working with the roach coaches, or somewhere else?

"He is working every day. Someplace different all the time. Right now roach coach."

He said something about that before I left today. Thank you, Madam, thanks.

"What place you go to now?"

The Side Car, maybe you've been there. I have a few friends that might still be hanging around. And Robeson goes there sometimes.

"Be careful, Tall Boy. Maybe a night for trouble."

"Look at this big motherfucker coming through the door, y'all," Luther said. "I believe it's none other than F.N.S. himself. We been hearing about you, Francis. Where you been hiding?"

I've been working Luther, Francis said, been working out on a ranch.

"Step back now y'all. This creazy cat might just combust at any moment. Somebody jump up here and buy this scarhead a cold one and a shot of gasoline."

I left the ranch late last night, Luther, and drove into Denver on the back roads.

"Don't tell me, let me guess it. There was a problem. Somebody did something, said something, and somebody got hurt."

Pindar, he never should've brought those guys in, Luther. I knew what they were going to do. So I set the operating room . . . I set it on fire, but I had a reason. He was going to try to cut my heart out, take the last of my blood.

"That might've been painful, for you and the people inside that operating room. Whatever happened to shooting somebody, like in the good old days? Maybe setting fires is the new shooting. But that wasn't the end of it, was it? I'm just looking at your face, Francis, and can see that wasn't the end of it. Fires and operating rooms."

At the old west town, which was on the far side of the ranch, I didn't have a choice, he had a gun, and he shot the coyote. I didn't feel like I had a choice.

"Two people already. It's starting to mount up. These sound like great stories with old west towns, guns, and coyotes. But not tonight, Francis, right? Not here, ok?"

I just came to have a beer, Luther, see you and everybody. I was on the 15 before to see Madam, have some noodles.

"How is Madam? I haven't seen her since we . . . since a while."

She's ok. We didn't talk about you. She's staying with Robeson now, in the furniture-store basement. That's where I am. Twins are there too, Alferd and Cross, though I haven't seen either of them.

"Let Omar in here, Francis. Omar, you see who's here? You remember Omar don't you, Francis?"

"Good to see you, Francis. Can I buy you something, a beer? Maybe take some of your money at eight-ball?"

Nice to see you too, Omar. How's your daughter? She ok now? Her legs better now? And I might have a few bucks so we can play. But it's in a big bill.

"She's fine, my girl. What with the physical therapy and the chemo. You was working out somewhere, didn't I hear Luther say that?"

Yeah, on a ranch that did different things. Regular ranch things and a strange kind of transplant place.

"You mean like cow transplants or sheep, that sort of thing?"

Nah, this was humans, organs, hearts, that sort of thing.

"Was it weird? Sounds a little weird."

It was weird. But the ranch was big, mostly nice. Beautiful country. Except the bad parts; it had some bad parts.

"Let me give you a token or two for the table," Luther said. "Y'all can play a couple games on the house. Francis, Omar, y'all want chips, pretzels, something to snack on?"

"I'm ok, Luther. I guess you heard they come around, Francis, haven't you?"

Robeson told me. Madam too. Have they been in here? Did they come in asking questions about me? Did they ask Luther to call if I came?

"They left a card with Luther. Told him if you showed up to give 'em a buzz. You want to break or you want me to?"

You go ahead, Omar. Let me ask Luther about the card. Did Omar get that right, Luther? Did the police leave a card?

"Detective. Skinny guy. Bald. Left me his card and I put it in the drawer. I'll get my glasses and read the name to you. Spradley, says here, Robert. Detective with Homicide for District 6."

"Your shot, Francis. You got the big ones."

Mind if I see that card, Luther? I'll put it here in my pocket while we're shooting. I want to look at it again.

"Well, ok, Francis. But don't forget to give it back before you leave, hear? This way I got a name if something ever happens; I'm not just calling a number with voicemail."

"Where was this ranch, Francis? I used to work out there

around Limon when I was a young man. It was still a lot of manual work then, hard work."

You know where Doveless is, Omar? North of Limon, back this way from Anton? It was near there.

"Doveless was an actual town, I remember that. You spend much time around that town or just stay at the ranch?"

Mostly at the ranch, Omar. I went down there last night, went down there to see someone I knew. But I didn't get to spend much time. Lots of work on the ranch. When we weren't doing one thing out there we were doing something else, transplants.

"You just scratched on the eight, Francis, but I'll let it go. Probably didn't get a chance to play much pool out there, did you? And what kind of place was it that did operations on humans. You said it wasn't no veterinary place, right?"

I guess I forgot about the eight ball. That a new rule? It was a different place, Omar, that's for sure. And I was being trained to be a transplant technician. I was right there helping out. I saw them putting them in and taking them out.

"You mean like hearts and livers, what else, kidneys, that sort of thing, pancreas?"

All of it. I even had to do some defib, if you know what that is.

"I do know what that is. My wife's mother had to have some of that. But it didn't help her none."

Any work you know about, Omar? Any place I can go and do some work, earn some money? Robeson told me about the bus thing.

"That's Alferd doing the bus. When it's nice like today, the car wash always needs people, long as you don't mind a few Mexicans."

Can I do work in the back, out of the way?

"They got people detailing tires in the back, but the only thing is you get all wet. They give you rubber boots and an apron but they don't help that much. They split the tips and you make a little more that way."

Luther said, "I'm watching out the window here, Francis, and I see two cops going in places. They're in the Greek's right now across the street and they just come out of the taco joint. You best cut for the hills, if you know what I mean. They'll be in here next looking around, asking questions. Maybe they don't know nothing about you, but they might try to get to know you."

Ok, Luther, I don't want to cause any trouble. I'll see you two another day. Robeson comes by, let him know I was here.

"Take care, Francis. It's going to be hard for y'all to stay out of the way and everything. I been on the run a couple times myself, and it's no life, know what I'm saying. You take care. Don't forget your noodles."

You're not just saying something to me, are you, about those police being around? You're on the up-and-up, aren't you?

"Come take a look. You think I'm kidding, come look out this window."

No, I trust you, Luther. I just was trying to have a little enjoyment among friends, that's all, an evening.

"Take care, Francis. Y'all take care, here."

3.

The door was unlocked and the note from Robeson said, "Francis, key is under the pillow on your bed, dude. Lock the door if you leave. Chancellor will be here tonight. Told the Twins you were around. They're excited to see you. Fridge is there if you have stuff and a microwave too. Might be late when I get in. The hound, man, watch for the hound."

The hound, Francis said to himself. I don't like having to watch for the hound all the time, worrying about who's around the corner, who might be coming after me. And I'd like to have what other people have, friends to talk to, even a. . . .

Francis lay down on the bed after putting the sheets and pillowcases on it and taking his shoes off. The bed was indeed too small, by a foot. He had only planned to rest for a minute but drifted off. When he roused he could hear the tail end of his breath rattling in his ears. Then there was noise, voices in the other room—the Twins. But because they sounded the same he couldn't tell them apart.

There was a little tap, a knock at the door.

The Twins said, "Francis, are you awake?"

And then they piled in, jumped on the bed and lay on top of him. They were wearing kimonos, open in front. They still looked like children; children's faces, children's bodies, and their voices were like kids.

"Where you been?" they said. "We've missed you, Bigamust."

They always made him laugh, the Twins, like puppies. Bigamust. They were a little, he didn't know what to say, different, that was the way Madam had raised them, but he liked them, and because he was feeling a little low, it was good to see them.

I've been out at the ranch, he said. And I've missed you too.

They wanted to know all about the ranch, the transplants, the old west town, and why he'd come back.

Trani and Van. Or Tran and Vani. Sometimes he got the names mixed up. And it was Vani who always wanted to give him a bath. He let her massage him. Head and face, chest, back, legs and feet. His feet hurt a lot. Vani especially liked to squeeze and rub his head with her tiny hands and with her boy-chest pressing against it. So nice, he thought. And they liked to take his clothes off. But not all of them.

Vani looked at his shoes and touched his feet.

"What size are these, Francis?"

Sixteen, he said.

"You should let people live in these shoes when you're not wearing them. We'll paint signs on the sides. Duplex for rent."

Vani, he said, you're so funny. What have you guys been doing? What have you been up to while I was gone? Madam says you've been modeling.

"And dancing. Should we show him?"

They stood together in the middle of the room and held their arms out, with their robes wide open. Then they began to sing a little song with their eyes closed. The dance was like two junior-high girls or unaccomplished ice skaters; like two kids playing in their room, picking things up, pointing, brushing past each other, pretending to stumble, dancing on the balls of their feet. Francis didn't know much about dancing, but it seemed like they were just practicing, fooling around.

They were out of breath when they'd finished, but they wanted to know what he thought. He clapped and clapped and stood up and said great, great, and they were happy and both cried.

Then a man with oversized glasses and a bow tie opened the door and stepped in. He was smallish, with no hair and a body like the Twins'. Plus he had a soft pointy face, but one like he meant business, or that he was in charge.

"If you aren't in over your head," he said, looking at Francis, "how do you know how tall you are? T.S. Eliot." Then he came closer and shook Francis's hand. "Edmund, as in the martyr, as in *King Lear*, as in California's governor, also known as Jerry, as in Sir the mountain climber and philanthropist. And who might you be, tall person?"

He had a small hand but a good grip.

"We call him Bigamust. That's Francis, our friend, Chan. We lived together and he took care of us in the apartment, protected us from the weirdos. Francis, this is Chan, the Chancellor of the college, also known as Edmund, but nobody calls him that."

"He's also father of the P-Tat," the Chancellor said, "maybe you've heard of it. The first short-term multi-modal cutaneous communication device, paper thin. Would you like to join us for dinner, Francis? The children and I are going someplace special, after they've re-clothed themselves."

"Yes, yes, we forgot. We're going to dinner. Chan is taking us to a place that serves food from Niger. Or is it Nigeria, Chan?"

"It's Niger, children. *Avec de la musique.* So let's be going or we'll never be gone."

While the Twins got ready the two men sat in the living room and talked, or tried. Chan told Francis all about his company and P-Tat, that it was ahead of its time when it came out, and that he would give him one if he wanted it.

Francis didn't actually want to go with them; he didn't want to go to the Niger restaurant and eat that food, whatever it was. He wanted to stay in his new room and think about things. But he went with them because they made a fuss, took him by the arms. The food was mostly veggies, lentils and different onion salads with cucumbers and tomatoes, and mutton.

And there indeed was music, from a kind of guitar, a drum, and a bent trumpet, and one of them singing mournful songs. The songs were in a language he'd never heard before, not French. Chan had said it was Hausa. The Twins got up to dance and they dragged Chan and Francis up with them. Chan drank several glasses of wine, the Twins shared a Dr. Pepper, and Francis drank a big glass of club soda.

When they sat down again, the Twins continued to dance in their junior-high, ice-skating way, which everybody and the band liked. Over the noise, Chan asked Francis if he had a job, if he was working. He didn't know what to say at first. He didn't know him that well and he started to say yes, he had a job, a good job at the car wash. But he told the truth, said no, he didn't have a job, but needed one.

"*Mon grand ami*," he said, looking at Francis closely, "would you like to go to work for me as my security? I need someone with a bit of size to look out for me. I was recently targeted at an event; there have been a few close calls. This is personal, beyond campus security. And the Twins think the world of you."

What would I have to do? Francis asked. What does your security do?

"We'd have to find some better clothes for a start, and get you *el corte de pelo*. Sometimes when you've done things that put you in the spotlight, others are resentful, jealous, if you know what I mean."

He didn't know what he meant, but said he did. And he didn't have any idea about being in the spotlight. Francis said he didn't want to do it, but Chan asked him to think about it, and the Twins told him to go ahead and do it after he told them he didn't want to.

"Security," the Chancellor said, "for someone like me, means keeping your eyes on movement, making sure those who intend to be rude or disagreeable or aggressive are kept at bay or are excluded and made to feel uncomfortable, escorted away. Do you have an idea now?"

Better, Francis said, but he still didn't know exactly what that meant.

Where will I make these rude people feel uncomfortable? Francis asked. At your house or like at big deals such as college parties or social events, and by following you around everywhere and riding in your car, maybe even driving it? Being in big groups makes me nervous.

"Most of the time," Chan said, "all you have to say is excuse me, excuse me, please step back, or excuse me please don't shout or put your hand on the Chancellor, or please follow me, it's time to leave. Don't you think you could do that?"

But I wouldn't want to have to rough people up, Francis said, and I wouldn't want to have to dress up all the time. I've never actually had to dress up that I can remember. Jeans and tees and a couple long-sleeve shirts, that's about it.

When they got back to the basement, the Twins went into their room to watch the big-screen TV, and Chan sat in the living room drinking more wine. He wanted to know where Francis had worked before and he told him about the ranch, including the transplant part.

"Out east, yes?" Chan asked. "Near the town of Doveless?"

That's right, Francis said, how did you know?

"I've met this Pindar," he said. "That's who owns it, isn't it?"

Yes, he said, Pindar owns the ranch. He wanted to blurt out about the fire, about the blood match, about the old west town. He'd been wanting to tell someone about what happened, but thought this was probably not the best time or the right person.

"He was at one time looking for investors. But it seemed a little too, what, *abbozzato* I think the Italians would say."

Whatever that meant, *abbozzato*, it didn't sound like the ranch. He wondered if staying up and talking to Chan would be part of his duties, in addition to security. He asked the Chancellor to excuse him, that he'd been up most of the previous night and was pretty tired, and that he needed to get to bed.

"Ummm," Chan said, nodding toward the Twins' room and gesturing with his wine, "as security everything will be confidential, is that understood, beginning tonight? Conversations, guests who might have been there, my actions?"

Yes, Francis said, everything confidential. And then he looked at him carefully, this smallish man who had a thing for the Twins, with his bow tie and glasses, who was a college Chancellor.

What was there to say? Francis thought. Of course he would be his security. He needed a job and didn't like the idea of being wet all day from cleaning tires.

Good night, Francis said, nice to meet you, and Chan said good night and shook his hand.

"I'll have someone call in the morning," he said. "My people, your people."

Francis wondered where they would call and who would be calling? It was late and he wanted to brush his teeth and go to bed. From the Twins' room he could hear low talking and the TV. Francis was so tired that he plopped down on the bed without taking off his clothes. And he wanted to tell Chan that the police might be looking for him and that it might not work. That he was insecure about being his security person.

But he shivered and turned over, adjusted the pillow, and was out.

That night he dreamed of the bear. He was running toward the city lit up in the distance, and he stopped occasionally to smell the air with his big nose, stopped to get his breath and his bearings. Then he went on running, running, closer and closer to the city.

4.

The Twins came into the room excited, woke Francis, and handed him the phone. His early morning dream had been about the basement, drifting around in an over-sized bed, like a magic carpet, and that it was so nice to be resting there. The Chancellor was calling from the college, and he wanted to get Francis signed up so he could work for him, there were events coming over the next month that he needed help with like student protests, a controversial neighborhood meeting, sports events, and even a faculty termination that could turn violent.

Robeson had mentioned earlier that the women's basketball team was sure to be in the finals, they hadn't lost a game, and they had a good chance of winning the title.

"Are you ok with all this?" the Chancellor asked.

How much? Francis asked.

"How about two-fifty."

A week? Francis asked.

"A day," he said, "and a thousand a week if it's more than a couple?"

Fine, Francis said, but. . . .

The Chancellor quickly put his assistant back on the phone and said she would collect some basic information, and that he would need to come over in the afternoon to sign documents. The assistant spoke with Robeson, told him to come get the card so he could help Francis buy clothes and a haircut.

When Francis went out into the big room, Robeson was warming something in the microwave and told him to hurry and get cleaned up, shave, so they could go and buy new clothes.

"Put some polish on those shoes too, man, so you look half decent with your clothes. We might have to get some of those too."

Francis tried to hurry while he was shaving, cut himself in a few places, and had to daub the spots with toilet paper.

When he'd finished eating cereal they went to a discount men's store, to the big and tall department.

"You play ball?" the clerk asked.

No, Francis told him, not knowing which kind of ball he meant. But he'd never played ball so it didn't matter.

"I should have guessed," he said, pointing at his feet. "Basketball players all have really nice shoes."

Robeson paid for the clothes and said Chan had asked if he had any pocket money.

I got a thousand bucks, Francis said. But it's a big bill and nobody wants to cash it.

"Give it to me, dude," Robeson said. "We'll get it cashed right now and you can pay some rent money."

They walked down the street, past a breakfast place, and into a bar called Doctor's. All the people there looked like they should have been somewhere else, possibly prison.

When Robeson showed the bartender the green bill, the bartender held it up and said, "Twenty on a thou," and crossed his arms.

"You ok with that, Francis? Dude wants twenty bucks to cash your thousand-dollar bill?"

Yeah, he said. That way I have something to spend.

In the car Robeson said, "You know why he cashed that bill and charged you?"

No, why? Francis asked.

"I'll tell you another day."

Around one o'clock they went to a sandwich shop with his new money and Robeson made him buy. Then he asked for a hundred for rent; he said he needed the money because not everybody else had paid. Francis said, No problem, and that he didn't mind, he was just glad to have found a place so easily.

After he'd gotten a haircut and was wearing the new clothes, Robeson told him to stand still so he could adjust his collar, check him out. He took a picture with his phone.

"You don't look half bad for a white man who's as pretty as Sonny Liston."

I dreamed about the bear last night, Robeson.

"Which bear would that be?"

The one that followed the train and lived at the ranch.

"Oh, you mean *that* bear?"

Yeah, he said, that bear.

"I got no idea what bear you're talking 'bout, man."

The bear that was there with me, and in the dream he was coming to the city.

"He's going to have a hell of a time when he gets to the city. So, you ready to help Chan out today? Either that or you can get on Alferd's bus and do the RTD thing. He gave me the sign today and told me which route it was going to be."

Which route is it?

"The 27, down off Yale."

I'm ready to help the Chancellor, but I'm not exactly sure what to do.

"We'll go back to his office and you can ask him. Mostly I think it's helping him avoid any potential conflicts, keeping the fuckin' strange people away."

Francis expected it to be busy and that he would have to fend people off left and right, but that didn't happen. For a few weeks he did a lot of sitting and standing and in the meeting with the neighbors, where the college had purchased the land all around them and planned to put in a new student union, they grumbled and shouted but didn't become too contentious. The faculty member who was expected to be violent, however, saved his anger and after a half-hearted argument, promptly went home and tried to hang himself in the spare bedroom, but failed.

It was during this period that Francis found time to begin his sessions with Dr. Glass at the Indigent Clinic, sometimes twice a week.

After the basketball quarterfinals, when it was determined that the women's team was indeed in the playoffs for the championship, Francis wondered what he would have to do.

"You're gonna have to be around a lot more, man," Robeson said, "that's what it means. Buy yourself a couple more white shirts."

Robeson was right and Francis began working longer days. On the day of the playoffs, when he got to the college, the Chancellor was in a meeting. His assistant told him to sit for a few minutes until he was finished. He came out but had to go right into another meeting. He suggested Francis go over to the field house and watch the women's team practice and he would join him later. Robeson met Francis along the way.

To get into the field house they had to have the guard at the door call the Chancellor's office; they wouldn't let them into the gym otherwise. When they got inside the first thing Francis noticed was that all the women were over six feet, except one. At Robeson's suggestion they sat courtside.

"These are Chan's special seats," Robeson said smiling. "And I want to get me a look at some big girls' asses, some basketball asses runnin' around, man. This is where you'll be sitting tonight."

Three of the five on the court, and half of the ones on the bench, were black, Francis noticed and he said something to Robeson about it.

"Couldn't help but see that, eh man? Big and black and beautious. You get a look at that tall one out there?"

Robeson was pointing to one of the players who was at least six-five.

"She's tearin' up the league, baby. Nobody can stop her. And she ain't afraid to get in people's faces neither."

Just then a ball flew into the stands and the tall black girl came chasing after it.

Robeson retrieved it and handed it to her.

"Robeson," she said and stood there looking at him.

"Poletta," he said. "What's the haps."

Then they bumped fists.

"Ain't nothin' to it, Robe," she said. "Who's your friend?"

Robeson looked at Francis and said, "This big cat is Francis. Francis this is Poletta."

Francis nodded and they shook. She held onto his hand for a second.

"You two boys gonna get off the sofa and come to the game tonight?" Poletta asked. "There gonna be some hoops this evenin', watch and see."

"This is the Chanmaster's special security detail," Robeson said. "He's got to be here. And I have to work."

"You gonna wish you had taken the night off, Robeson," she said. "These white girls are fixin' to find out what in your face is about."

Poletta returned to practice and Robeson slapped Francis on the back.

"I think that Negro gal kinda likes you."

What makes you say that? I thought she was your friend.

"I dream about Poletta, but she prefers her men tall, not babies like me."

Another thing Francis noticed about Poletta was that she had green eyes, not dark like Robeson's. And she had large hands but slender fingers. And that she had beautiful teeth. And that she kept looking at him every chance she got.

When they were nearly done practicing, Francis got a call from the Chancellor's office for them to go back. There would be a dinner between the officials of the two schools before the game, the administrators and faculty, and the Chancellor wanted Francis to be there, in the background.

"They also serve who only stand and wait," the Chancellor said after he'd explained what was going to happen. "From 318."

From 318, Francis repeated to himself, as if I should know what the hell that means.

He thought maybe he meant the year the author wrote it, but maybe not. That seemed like a long time ago. He wanted to ask Robeson if Poletta would be at the dinner, but didn't want to be embarrassed, and then he went and sat in a chair in the hall.

The dinner was just an early afternoon light supper. Small steaks, green beans, something else, cake. The Chancellor walked with the chief of the other school and they talked in almost a whisper. Lots of students approached and he shook their hands. Francis walked behind and watched. The Chancellor was definitely a hand shaker.

While they were walking, a student with bright hair stopped the Chancellor and raised his voice, got close and shook his finger. Francis stood next to the student and squeezed his arm. The Chancellor said, "That's all right, Francis. This student is just exercising his First Amendment rights, peaceably, yes?"

To Francis the student shouted, "Fuck you, mother-fucker" and stomped away. He didn't like it, and wanted to go after him, but he was positive that wouldn't look good. It was his first time acting like security, and he wasn't sure how he felt about it.

At the dinner, out of the corner of his eye, Francis watched for Poletta, thinking she might be there, but she never appeared, nor did any of her teammates. Just the school officials.

After the dinner and filling out more forms at the Chancellor's office, Francis and Chan had a coffee in the library and walked to the field house. The Chancellor talked to Francis, in between interruptions, and told him what was going to happen that night: introductions at center court, the game, the trophy ceremony, the party after. Francis was supposed to sit behind him and watch. People would come and go during the game, the Chancellor said, sit down next to him, but none for too long. And if that student with the bright hair came again, he was to escort him out, but not too forcefully.

For about a minute Francis paid attention to who came and went. Mostly white men with ties sat down and some women in black. The other team was announced and they ran out and shot the basketball around, dribbled and stretched.

Then the lights went off and on and the college band marched onto the floor in maroon uniforms. Ladies and gentlemen, the announcer said, your hometown, five-time champion baaasketbaaall wommmen. And Poletta and the rest of the team came flying out with the lights flashing and the band playing real loud and the drums going boom-boom-boom.

The team did a lot of dunking and fancy shooting, dribbling between their legs, while the band continued to play. The girls on the other team stood around and watched. It was a show and a half and Poletta led them. At the tipoff she tapped the ball to her teammate and it seemed from that moment on the game was over. The other team looked like little girls and midgets, and it took them a while to figure out what was going on.

But Poletta was beautiful the whole time, shouting orders to teammates, blocking the other school's shots, soaring like some kind of bird force. She'd scored 38 points before it was over and she could have been wearing a cape. The students chanted Po-Po-letta, Po-Po-letta and danced and marched in a big line around the court. There was no doubt who the national champion was and no doubt who was in charge of the team that night.

Before the end, in the last minute, Poletta called a timeout and dribbled the ball over to the Chancellor. She handed it to him and pointed at Francis: "See you at the party," she said, and then tossed a new ball to her teammate, who dunked it.

"Poletta Odom," the Chancellor said, "*il miglior fabbro*, and a person you obviously have some knowledge of, yes?"

Oh, only through Robeson and this afternoon at practice, Francis said.

"You'll get a chance to meet and talk with her face to face at the victory celebration, and there most certainly will be a celebration."

The game was over quickly and the women won by a large score; the other team was embarrassed. The Chancellor shook all their hands and posed for pictures, one of him hugging Poletta. With a ladder the women cut the net from the hoop.

The Chancellor spoke to the coach for a minute, patted her on the back, and then signaled it was time to leave.

"Any difficulty tonight?" the Chancellor asked Francis. "Any problems with the rabble?"

None, he said shaking his head and trying to act like a security person.

"Snap, big guy," the Chancellor said, "nothing to it."

At the party, there were lots of college people, both teams, fans, teachers, plenty of food, and a band. Alcohol too. Some of the food Francis had never heard of before. Baba ghanoush, for instance, made from roasted eggplant, and which sounded and looked like something from a baby's diaper. Plus the biggest bowl of avocado dip he'd ever seen. But no Poletta.

On the way over, the Chancellor told him to move around the room, look for people who didn't belong, and wait till the end to eat. There was regular campus security in the room too, but Francis didn't talk to them.

Even though students were not supposed to smoke marijuana on campus, lots of them were outside smoking and they smelled like burning leaves when they came back in. When Francis looked out the window to see what was going on, he saw Poletta, kissing one of her teammates and smoking a joint. Everyone else was in jeans, but she was wearing a bright red dress, puffy, and very short. Her hair was tied up in two buns, one on either side of her head, with red ribbons.

She saw him, finally, and waved, leaned over and told him to come out, that they were getting stupid on the balcony. Francis looked around the room to see if he could find the Chancellor. He was having a conversation and had his back to him.

Poletta pulled him out the door and put her arms around him, kissed him big on the mouth.

"It was so close," she said, shaking and pretending to be upset. "I was worried you and the Chan might leave. Did you like it?"

Francis said he really liked it, especially her part.

Poletta smelled as if she'd put on fragrant powder and when he looked at her bright red lips against her smooth, dark skin, it felt like, he wasn't sure, like some kind of vision, like a scene in a movie, and he had to clear his throat.

"Let's go somewhere secret, dad," she said, "let's bust the fuck out."

I've got to stay with the Chancellor, he said, I'm his special security. I can't leave.

"Don't you have some place we can go, Tallboy? Where the queen of hearts can get out of her costume?"

Poletta began to dance, hands up and shimmying, and

then she put her hands to her ears, rocking her head, like she was listening to headphones.

I used to break into these big houses that were under construction, he said. They were almost finished and they even had carpeting. I know where one is. Want to go there?

"Dude, that's the motherfucking place I'm talking about. Can we stay the night? Just tell Chan baby there's a major security problem, a big group of pissed off fans gonna crash the party if they don't find out what happened to Poletta; you think he better leave now."

What happened to Poletta? Francis asked. Did something happen to you?

"The cops, they went lookin' for the red queen, all that disturbance she made tonight, searching high and low, but she escaped, the queen flew, baby. And they have called out the militia; they gonna bring it down if they don't find her."

Francis went back inside and while the Chancellor was listening to someone talking, he whispered in his ear that he thought they should go, that there were angry students on the way, something about the cops and Poletta, and there was a chance it could turn violent. The Chancellor apologized and gathered himself, saying goodbye to this person and that person as he exited.

While they drove, the Chancellor talked about the game, how great it was for the school, and that he'd won the bet with the president of the other college. Then he abruptly shifted and began to sing:

Alla en el rancho grande, alla donde vivia
Habia una rancherita, que allegre me decia
Que allegre me decia

"Where did you say the ranch you worked on was located?" he asked. "Near Doveless?"

Yeah, Francis said, near Doveless, out east.

"My sister works in that town, somewhere in a café. She's always liked driving around out on the prairie, especially when she was having trouble. She's got a Ph.D. in psychology but has never used it. If I gave you money, do you think you could find the café and deliver it to her?"

Sure, Francis said, I think I know which one that is. But he didn't want to ask her name. He wanted the Chancellor to tell him.

"The Twins won't be here right away," the Chancellor said, "can you stay and talk to me? You can have my car when they come. How does that sound? And you've been doing a good job for the first few weeks, especially keeping a close eye on Poletta."

Yeah, he said, sure, I could hang around. But he badly wanted to leave, to say no, to not stay with the Chancellor until the Twins came, and to go and meet Queen Poletta.

But the Chancellor needed someone to talk to that night and he'd had a few glasses of champagne. He wanted to talk about how much the faculty at the college were whiners, that the administrators were incompetent, and that the students were sub-par. He said he'd donated millions to the school, but no one had yet thanked him for his gifts. And someone had started a rumor that he was sleeping with the students.

Just before midnight the Twins let themselves in and were glad to see them. They both hugged the Chancellor like a lost uncle, then came and jumped on Francis. After the two men had given the report on the game, the Chancellor gave Francis a signal that meant he was done for the night; he was free to go, and he hurried out the door.

At the campus Francis drove by the building where the after-party was, but the lights were out and nobody was around. Poletta had told him to come to her dorm, so he drove there. Girls were out front lounging around, but no Poletta. Francis put the window down and called out to a group of them. They were leery but came a little closer.

Anybody seen Poletta Odom? Is Poletta Odom around?

They looked at each other and shouted weirdo, fucking creep, and monster at him, then flipped him off. The Chancellor's car had a special sticker so Francis parked and turned the radio on for a while, then turned it off so it didn't drain the battery. When he got sleepy he scooted the seat back. It was still a tight fit and he had to move over to the passenger side to stretch his legs.

Francis could feel himself wandering and at some point he knew he was asleep and that he'd eventually have to rouse himself and go home. When he really began to dream, the red came in big strokes and sloshes, like from a giant paint brush and a bucket, but there were no people, only red paint everywhere on a glass dividing wall.

And then the knocking came. Steady, steady, until he decided it wasn't part of the dream, and he struggled to wake.

5.

Just as soon as I drop the Chancellor off, he told Poletta, I'll come back to get you. She had written her address down, Buckley Hall, and kissed him.

"I'll be waitin', Tallboy," she said. "You better not stand this queen up."

The Chancellor went along with him and excused himself from the gathering.

"Are you sure we need to leave?" he asked. "There's still plenty of smoked salmon to be eaten and important discussions to be had, like how much more we're going to have to pay the coach now."

Francis said he was sure, that the students had told him the protestors were on their way, and some might be armed.

"What happened to our girl, the star of the game?"

You mean Poletta? She's outside with her friends. I kept an eye on her. But the students were worried something happened to her, that she'd been arrested or kidnapped.

"She's a charmer but a terrible student," the Chancellor said as they hurried to the car. "We do everything we can to keep her in school. But she loves her teammates, some more than others, and she could have gone anywhere."

Francis wanted to tell the Chancellor how great Poletta looked dressed as the queen of hearts, and how beautiful the red looked against her dark brown skin, that she'd kissed him twice on the mouth, and that he was going to meet her as soon as he dropped him off. But he realized he might not appreciate the story he'd made up about violent protestors, once he'd figured it out, and that he'd made up that story.

Well, Francis said dragging it out, she seems like a nice person and a good athlete.

Smiling, the Chancellor said, "You don't mind that she's so . . . so . . . mahogany, so sepia, do you?"

Mind, Francis said looking at him kind of strange, why would I mind?

"Ever play sports as a kid?" the Chancellor asked. "You look like you might've played sports. I was always too small, even to be the water boy."

We moved too much, Francis said, and things just kept happening at the homes we were in so I never got involved.

"Someday you'll have to tell me about that part," the Chancellor said, patting Francis on the shoulder.

The knocking sound was campus security at the window. Francis opened the door and almost fell onto the pavement.

"This the Chancellor's car isn't it?" the officer said looking in the windows. "Would you mind stepping out of the vehicle?"

Francis got out and the officer shined his light inside.

"You his driver?" he asked. "I haven't seen you around. What's your name?"

No, I'm his new security, Francis Stein. I'm waiting on somebody. A friend of the Chancellor's.

"Ok," he said, looking him over. "Sorry to disturb you. Drive safe."

When Francis started the car to leave, he could see a group of students coming across the lawn. Poletta was in the center of the pod, and they were all dancing, singing, celebrating. Poletta had scooped her short dress up in her arms and her lacy pink underwear was showing. She was barefoot.

Standing by the car Francis hoped she would see him, but he didn't wave or try to get her attention. Just before the group entered the dorm, though, Poletta turned and looked out in his direction. She sent her friends on inside and walked toward him.

"Tallboy, Tallboy," she called out, "is that you?"

He waved and smiled, shrugged his shoulders.

"What was you gonna do, man, let the queen just travel on past?"

She hugged him and kissed him all over the face.

You still want to do something? Francis said. It's kinda late.

"Yeah, is there someplace we can go, get a drink, get wasted? I thought everything would be closed in this city."

There's a bar I go to, the Side Car, that stays open late. But you have to go in the back.

"These all white people?" she asked.

Mixed, he said. But some are kind of hustlers.

"Sounds like my kind of place. This your car?"

Chancellor's, but he let me use it after I dropped him off.

"He's got a thing for those Twins, don't he?"

Yeah, I think so. Not sure exactly what it is, though.

When they got to the bar, there were lots of people inside, but the noise stopped when they saw Poletta. She nodded to folks and walked right up to the bar, adjusted her bra with both hands, then ordered shots of tequila for the two of them, thought twice about it and ordered shots for everyone. They gathered around her like she was a celebrity and gulped the shots down.

"You got money, Tallboy? We gonna need some money before this night's over."

Francis waved at Luther and told him to run a tab.

"Hold it, hold it," she said to the group and made them all be quiet. "Anybody 'cept Tallboy here go to the game tonight?"

No one raised their hands.

"Motherfucking whities," she said. "The small college finals were right here in your town and we won the goddamn thing, did we win, Tall?"

They won big time, he said.

From in the back someone yelled "What was the score?"

"A jillion fuckin' to nothin'," she said laughing large and wagging her head.

The old man standing next to Poletta growled "Jagers all around."

"Play some music," Poletta shouted to Luther behind the bar. "And not no Barry Manilow."

"How about Rihanna?" Luther asked.

"You ain't got no Rihanna," she said. "Let me see."

"My wife," Luther said, holding up the CD. "She likes her."

"Aight," Poletta said, throwing her Jager down, "play 'What's My Name'."

The song began 'Ooh na na, what's my name' and Poletta danced and picked it up.

"Po-Po-letta, what's my name." Then she sang it twice and pointed to the group.

"Po-Po-letta, that's your name."

"What's my name, y'all, what's my name?"

"What's her name, y'all, what's her name"

"Po-Po-letta, that's my name, Po-Po-letta, ax me a-gain."

Back and forth they went on singing even after the song was over, her calling out and them responding. And Po-Po-letta had a big, churchy singing voice.

"Ok, y'all," she said waving her hands to get them to stop. "Here's a good one for you. What do you call three short white men surrounded by ten big-ass black men?

Somebody said, "Fucked," and Poletta said, "Nah, baby. Refs in the NBA."

When the laughter died down she said, "And what do you call a black dude with a million white friends?"

Somebody said a banker, and Poletta said, "Mr. Obama, sir."

Poletta leaned against the bar with her elbows and asked Francis to buy yet another round. As Luther was pouring the shots, two policemen came in the back door. One stood by the exit and wouldn't let people out; the other asked to see everybody's I.D.s.

"Put this hat on and look short," Luther said to Francis, and handed him a baseball cap with NY on the front.

The Hispanic cop, the I.D. checker, asked Luther how it was that he was still serving drinks at 2:20 in the morning?

"I'm thinking there was some kind of law about that, wasn't there?" the officer asked Luther.

Luther said it was a private party to celebrate the college winning the game and the national title.

"What was the score of that game?" the cop asked.

Poletta looked at him and mouthed "Seventy-one to forty-eight."

"Seventy-one to forty-eight," Luther said.

"I didn't know you liked basketball that much, Luther," the cop said.

"Special game. You had to pay for it on TV. We wanted to see the college's star. Probably a first-round draft pick in the WNBA."

The second cop wandered around the room checking I.D.s and stopped in front of Poletta.

"Nice outfit, miss. What's it supposed to be?"

"Queen of hearts," Poletta said stepping up to him. "D'you like it, officer?"

"A little too red for me," he said. "Does a big girl like you happen to have any I.D. on her?"

"I must've left my purse back at the house," she said.

"That you they were talking about in the game?"

"That's me," Poletta said, shaking his hand with her big hand.

"Who's driving this college car, the Chancellor's car out here?"

I am, Francis said to the officer. Is it parked illegally?

"I believe it's time for you two to go, isn't it?" the officer said looking Francis over. "Time for the queen of hearts to return to her palace with her tall escort."

The officer who was at the door opened it and let them out, but made everyone else stay. He pointed and started to ask Francis a question, but then closed the door.

"Drive around a little bit, Tallboy," Poletta said when they'd gotten in the car. "I don't want to go to that house yet. I got a chill, know what I'm sayin'."

For a while they were quiet as Francis drove down one street after the other. Poletta turned the heat on then the radio, and after a few minutes turned the radio back off. She put one of the Chancellor's violin CDs on and made a face. When she was warm she unbuckled her seatbelt, scooted as close as she could, and put her head on Francis' shoulder. As they headed east, away from the streetlights and out onto the prairie, she put his hand between her legs and began to moan, then cry.

Poletta, Francis said, Poletta, let's go back to the house, and when she nodded he drove to the new house in the nice neighborhood not far from the college. He parked next to the garage in the back and checked to see if they could get in before he waved at her. The Chancellor had blankets in the trunk and he got them and laid them on the floor.

"Can we turn on any of these lights?" she asked.

No lights, Francis said, the neighbors will call the cops for sure and we'll be in a shitload of trouble.

"Got anything to eat here? I didn't have any of that food at the party, and ain't had anything since before the game."

I got a bag of cheese popcorn in the car, he said.

"Go get it, Tall, and we can smoke a little of this weed somebody give me."

Even though they didn't have any lights on, with the street lamps and little lights in the house, they could see each other well enough after their eyes adjusted. When he got back from the car, Poletta had her clothes off and was playing music from her phone and dancing.

"You know how to dance, Tallboy? Can you move that big booty?"

Poletta had rolled a thick joint, almost as big as a cigar, and she took a drag and handed it to Francis. She danced around him, and he tried to dance, but he was uncoordinated. She laughed and pointed and danced right through from one song to the other.

"Why you still got your clothes on, Tall?"

She began to undress him and started with his new shoes.

"These are some big feets, Tall," she said taking his socks off and massaging his toes and heels. "I hope it's true, baby, what they say about big feets."

What do they say about big feets? he asked.

"Tall, you must be from the country," she said, "'cause everybody knows what big feets means."

Big feets, he said to himself, big feets. No idea.

"You think we could take a shower? Is the hot water on here?"

He went to the sink and checked the water. There was hot.

Poletta danced up the stairs and Francis checked the front door just to be sure. Standing in the middle of the big room, he listened to the creaking house noise and the shower water moving in the pipes. Poletta called out Tall, Tall, you comin'? and he walked to the back door and was about to lock it. When he did, he could see the flashlight shining through the door window and the nob turning slowly. He hid in an open broom closet and wanted to run up the stairs or call out, but it was too late. The officer was already inside, and he'd drawn his gun.

Francis had to hunker into the closet and the cop walked the other way, through the kitchen and then out into the dining room. Upstairs he could hear the door of the shower opening and closing and Poletta laughing and walking through the house.

The cop heard her too and crouched behind the sofa.

"Tall," she called out as she started down the stairs, "Tall, you never guess what I found."

Poletta, Poletta, Francis whispered, and maneuvered to be able to intercept her and step in front of the cop. But when she got to the bottom of the stairs, the policeman cocked his gun and yelled "Drop it."

She was carrying a big tube of caulk for sinks and showers in a metal holder. Poletta was smiling and she held it up as if to shoot Francis, but the look on her face was confused and she was very surprised to hear someone's voice other than his.

At the same moment, Francis stepped out from hiding and heard the crack, the explosion, and the officer firing twice at Poletta, hitting her square in the chest and on the right side above her eye. She made a small noise that sounded like a painful eh. The cop pointed his gun at Francis and then Poletta when she crumpled to the floor, and went back and forth.

"What's that in her hands," he screamed, his arms shaking. "Is that a weapon? That's an automatic weapon."

Francis went to Poletta without waiting and the officer cocked his gun again.

In a shrill voice he said, "Step away from her, step back."

But as soon as the officer moved toward her and looked at what he'd done, Francis knocked the pistol from his hand and tackled him. He was strong for a chunky man, but in just a moment, after plenty of struggle, it was over, he was limp and Francis let go of his neck. Francis got the officer's gun and fired a shot into his chest to make sure it was finished.

Jesus, Francis said, Jesus, when he got close and looked at Poletta. She was dead and there was blood everywhere and a stream of white caulk across her stomach, like a smiley face, just below her chest wound.

Francis didn't know whether to stay and call 9-1-1 or carry her out to the car and drive fast to the emergency room. When he looked at her again, though, lying naked and bloody, and after he called her name and put his hand on her head, it was clear no kind of medical help could save her.

But he didn't want anyone to see her there like that, so he took her upstairs to the glass shower and rinsed her off. When they were finished he found the red outfit and put it back on her. Blood continued to drip on the carpet, but at that point he didn't give a damn what happened to the house.

In his arms he carried her into each of the rooms and was crying. He said he was sorry again and again, that it was his fault, that the house was his idea, and that he hoped she could forgive him.

But he needed to ask a different question: Poletta, what should I do now? He didn't want to leave her, but it was clear with her being dead and with the dead policeman, there was going to be an enormous amount of difficulty ahead.

She told him: "Take the gun, leave the caulking tube, put the keys in the car, and get away, dad, far away."

And the house, what should I do about that?

"Never mind about the fuckin' house, get the hell out of there."

In the back yard there was equipment for landscaping. And a big can of fuel next to the port-a-potty. Francis quickly splashed some of it on the outside walls of the house and then went inside. Every room got a good dose of it, and he poured some on the officer.

But Poletta, he couldn't bring himself to deface her in any way, and he didn't want to leave her for people to find and bother. So he took her to the roof, there was a wooden deck on top, and he wrapped her in one of the blankets he'd found. He wanted to stay with her, but it wasn't possible. A touch of the sun was coming, and he kissed Poletta and said goodbye.

From a block away, you could already see the flames leaping into the sky and hear glass breaking and things exploding. It took a little while for the sound of the fire trucks to disturb the early morning, and Francis wanted to stop them, tell them it was too late, tell them to let it burn. But he needed to be gone, to think about where he would hide, to stay out of the way. Plenty of places in the mountains with empty cabins and condos. Some old buildings in the city, too, but lots of junkies and danger.

How did we go so quickly from a basketball game and party to having a good time at the Side Car, Francis wondered, to driving out on the prairie, to watching Poletta spinning around at the expensive house, to the cop shooting her, killing her? How did that happen? Why did it have to happen? One thing after the other, and so many things. Piling up and piling up. Since the beginning, since the Great Grandfather and the Doctor. The story of the Steins.

6.

In a big voice the pastor had begun praying, which Francis appreciated because he didn't want to be heard or seen. He thought if he could be anonymous and slouch in, with an NY hat and a coat with the collar turned up, that would be the way. The men and a few women were standing around the edge of the room with their heads bowed waiting for the serving line to start. The pastor was talking about Psalm 116: 1-2, loving the Lord because He heard your voice, heard your cry for mercy. This was the Christian pancake breakfast that was put on every Friday at the shelter. Francis hadn't had anything to eat since the afternoon before and thought it would be pretty safe to hang out there for a while.

When the pastor finished and people lined up, they turned the TV back on but muted it. Right away, in the middle of the breaking news, there was the Chancellor's picture and he was standing in front of an incinerated house, the new house, with a quote under him that said: "He came highly recommended." Then there was a fuzzy picture of Francis.

The anchor asked the Chancellor serious questions and their mouths moved, but the sound remained off. "On-going Arson/Double Homicide Investigation" the story was head-lined. There was a number to call if you had any information, and Francis's picture came up and completely filled the screen.

The man ahead of him in line was watching the TV, and Francis turned away and asked what happened in that story, what was the deal?

"Guy and his girlfriend break into a new house, they get high, he shoots his girlfriend during an argument, and when the cop comes to investigate he shoots him too, then catches the house on fire, burns that sucker down with both those people in it. They got a full-scale manhunt going on."

When Francis looked around the room no one was watching him, and only a few people were watching the TV. He was thinking that if he could find a way to hitch a ride out of town, up into the mountains, he would do it. Even if he had to pay a little money.

To that same guy Francis said Know anybody who's going up to the mountains today?

"I might be later on," he said. "Got any money for gas? My tank's on empty."

I could give you a few bucks, Francis said. How far you going?

"Maybe as far as Breck. That work for you?"

Where should I meet you? Francis asked.

"Know where that station is at Alameda and Broadway?"

The Conoco?

"Yeah."

What time?

"Ten-thirty. How about you give me the money now so I can put gas in the car and we can be ready to go?"

Francis thought about it and said he'd give him five now and five when he saw him.

"If you're late I'll leave without you."

A minute later, before he could finish his pancakes, a blind man with a cane and aviator sunglasses swept his way over and sat down across from him.

"How was it?" he asked.

How was what? Francis said.

"The heat," he said.

What heat? Francis said.

"That house must've gotten pretty hot. What'd you use, gas? That's the only way to get 'em goin' before the trucks get there. The bad news is you gotta get away before it gets roarin', can't even watch, cause if you do they nab you."

No idea what you're talking about, Francis said.

"I used to use chemicals when I was a torch," he said. "Put the fire downstairs by the heater and sometimes they couldn't tell. You got any money on you?"

For what? Francis said.

"Thought you might want to make me a loan. Let's start with a hundred. How does a hundred sound?"

Not too good. Why would I want to make you a loan for a hundred dollars?

"To keep me from calling the cops right now. What say?"

How about if I give you ten bucks?"

"That'll buy you about ten minutes, starting in about thirty seconds."

Francis gave him the ten bucks and gulped the last of the pancakes down. When he got to the sidewalk he could hear the sirens coming in his direction. He hid in the parking lot and then ran down the alley in the direction of the Conoco station. He was an hour early but something told him the Breckinridge ride wasn't going to be there anyway. And when 10:30 came and went he knew for sure.

While Francis was standing there trying to figure out what to do, every time a white vehicle that resembled a patrol car passed by, he jumped behind the building. And an actual cop did stop and he thought shit, that's it, but the officer used the restroom and got a soda.

Francis had to use the restroom himself and when he went inside, the clerk looked at him suspiciously. Maybe she just wanted me to buy something, he said to himself, or maybe she knows. When he came out of the restroom she smiled and asked where she knew him from.

I don't know, he said, maybe church.

"Ha," she said, "it's from the club isn't it? You work the door."

Which club? he asked.

"What d'you mean? The Sanctuary, of course. Didn't we have a little thing one night? Weren't you my slave when my friends didn't show?"

I don't think so. You've got me mixed up with somebody else. But I have a question for you. Know anybody going up to the mountains? I need a ride pretty quick. And I can help pay for gas.

"Stand outside and ask people, you'll find someone. Lots of people get on the interstate from here and then go right up to the mountains on 70."

For thirty minutes Francis stood outside asking if anyone was going up to the mountains, but no one was, or they didn't want to say. Then the clerk came back out and looked at him again.

"Now I know," she said. "I saw your picture on TV. That was you wasn't it?"

Yeah, he said, that was me.

"Did you start the fire?" she asked.

Yeah, he said, I started the fire.

"Did you kill those people, the cop and that black chic?"

The cop killed Poletta, and I killed the cop. He shot her twice for nothing.

"Watch out because the cops are always coming in here

getting sodas. They get 'em free. You gotta be gone in a few minutes. It's too dangerous for me, and if they start shooting. Sorry about that."

No problem, he said.

When he asked a woman if she was going to the mountains she hesitated, then said she was, but wondered if he could drive.

"Got any money?" she asked.

I can help out with a little gas money, he said.

"Gas is taken care of, sweetheart. I'm gonna need a six-pack and I'm short five."

At the liquor store the woman told him to stay with the car, that the doors didn't lock. Then she asked if he needed something. He told her he was ok, maybe some beef jerky. When she came out she only had the six-pack.

"No beef jerky," she said. "I only had enough for the beer. My choice was a cheap twelve-pack or a good six-pack. Just so you know, I got DUIs and that's why you're driving. I don't normally pick men up at the gas station."

As they were driving, the woman monopolized the conversation and spoke in a rat-a-tat style, and whenever Francis started to talk she talked over him and cut him off.

Do you live . . . ?

"I work in Silverthorne at the factory stores and I drive back and forth, share a house up there with ski folks. Rent is off the charts."

Are you an . . . ?

"I work on the floor of the alligator store, assistant manager, do their books and admin, take care of returns. Used to be an attorney."

How long have you . . . ?

"I been living up here for three years, working at this store for just six months, move around a lot. Seems like I just start to get comfortable and the next thing is I get sick or get into it with somebody or one of my roommates bails and I don't have the cash."

Are you originally . . . ?

"Kansas, I'm from Ford, Kansas. Written on both sides of the sign, but I been in Denver a while, a few years."

Would you like to listen . . . ?

"Yeah, sure, play some of that oldies shit. Whatever you want, just not too loud. This is how I manage the alligators, keep them in the Everglades."

Do you usually . . . ?

"I'd offer you a beer, dude, but I'm gonna need this whole six-pack, sorry hon."

How far . . . ?

"Careful about your speed and changing lanes cause the cops got my plates on a list and they stop me all the time."

Do you have . . . ?

"I got a brother in Denver I stay with. Big house with a basement, and I got my own room with a private bath. Not too bad."

Got any shirts in my . . . ?

"What's a big guy like you doing up here anyway? You don't look like a skier. Where's your car? Hard to be in the mountains without a car or pickup."

Are you much of a . . . ?

"I'm gonna have to let you off near Dillon, near the lake, 'cause that's near where I live, up the hill."

It took them an hour to get there on the interstate and as they got closer she told him for a big person he didn't talk much. She also finished the six-pack and then rinsed with mouthwash and spit out the window. A few blocks from the actual drop-off by the lake, a sheriff's deputy turned on his lights and pulled them over in a parking lot.

"Whatever he says, no matter what," the woman told him quickly, "say you haven't had anything to drink."

47

But I haven't had anything to. . . .

"Put your window down, he's out there now."

The officer knocked on the window, and Francis tried to put it down, but the motor didn't work.

"Push down on it," the woman said, "it's been acting up."

Finally the window went down with him pushing it.

"Can I see your license, proof of insurance, and your registration?"

The woman handed Francis the registration and her insurance card. He handed both of them to the officer. The officer looked through what Francis gave him and then asked for his driver's license.

I left it in Denver, he said, sorry about that.

"All right," the officer said, "step out of the vehicle please."

When he got out, the officer sniffed the inside of the car and asked if someone had been drinking.

No sir, Francis said.

"And your last and first name, let's start there."

Francis N. Stein, he said, and got ready to run away along the lake. As soon as his name came up on the computer, he knew he'd be put in handcuffs and hauled away.

"Was he violating the law in any way?" the woman in the car yelled. "Did he break any laws? I'm an attorney, you know."

"No, ma'am, he didn't. Are you the owner of this car? Are you Ms. Albers?"

The woman unbuckled her seat belt and started to get out of the car.

"Please, ma'am, stay in the car. Do not get out of the vehicle."

"Well, what the hell?" she said in her drunken voice.

"All right, sir," the officer said suddenly, handing Francis the insurance and registration, "you're free to go. Sorry for any trouble."

Francis watched the deputy walk carefully to his car and put it in reverse. The officer waited for them to leave and the woman, Ms. Albers, said, "Shit, now you're gonna have to drive me all the way home and then to work. Something happened there but I can't quite figure out what."

Without looking in the mirror or around them, Francis drove slowly across the parking lot. When another deputy appeared in the distance he said, Goddamn it to hell.

"Is there something you're not telling me?" the woman asked lighting a cigarette.

There's a lot I'm not telling you, he said.

A third deputy blocked the exit onto the street and Francis turned the car around and stomped on the gas. A small embankment and rail separated them from the frozen lake, but he thought it was worth a try. It was the only thing he could see to do, besides ramming one of their vehicles.

It was clear the officer had found Francis's name on his computer and called in reinforcements. If he got out of the car and ran, they would probably shoot him. If he cleared the embankment and didn't get stuck, he could drive out onto the lake, maybe make it to the other side before they drove around. If he didn't want to drive out onto the lake, he could follow the weedy path around the perimeter in the car.

To the frightened woman, Francis ran his hands through his hair and said motherfuckinsonofabitch.

The woman quickly tried to put her window down but instead puked on the inside of the glass.

At first the car hung up on the edge of the embankment, but when he rocked it and gunned the motor, somehow it broke loose. The rail broke loose, too, and flew up and clipped the hood.

Get out, Francis shouted at the woman, I'm driving onto the lake. She looked at him like he was crazy and when he bared his teeth, she said, "Ok, ok."

Even though it was springtime, Lake Dillon still had below freezing temperatures at night and part of the day. The lake was hard near the outer edge but in the middle it might not have been that thick. Slowly Francis drove the car and could immediately hear a crunch-cracking sound and the ice giving way. Behind him he could see the woman running and hear the deputies yelling. One of them was holding a rifle.

The car seemed to sink a little as Francis moved, and he thought for sure he'd get stuck. But he drove away quickly from the shore even though the cracking continued, like soft breaking glass, but he didn't fall through. The deputies tried to shoot out the tires and the back window and he had to duck down, but he didn't stop.

Halfway across the lake, Francis thought he might have a chance of getting away. The car was whizzing along even though all the windows, including the front, were gone, and there were bullets zinging everywhere.

But not surprisingly, the lake suddenly opened up, maybe from the sun or just a warm spot, and swallowed the car. As quick as that, the cold, cold water enveloped him, and he wondered how he would get out. Even though the cold didn't affect him like it did other people, the water took his breath away. And making it to the other side wasn't as big of a concern as getting back to the surface.

It took him a minute, he had to squeeze out the side window of the car, and he thought his chest was going to explode or he was going to gulp the frigid water and drown. But just as the colored lights behind his eyes began to blink, he burst to the surface and started to slide himself along the ice. He wasn't as big a target that way, but he could still hear the crack-crack of their shots. Though he wasn't as susceptible to the cold, he'd gotten soaked to the skin and that made a difference.

As he scratched along on the ice, he could see from where he was the lights of the other deputies' cars making the wide circle around the lake. He could also see places where it was possible to stand and run, and where he had to crawl again. But the first time he ran, he felt a sharp pinch in the back of his arm and something in his leg, but almost no blood appeared. And he didn't have a choice anyway except to continue, to stumble-skip along.

The far shore got closer and closer, but it seemed to take him longer, and by the time he'd reached the narrow beach, he was so tired he wanted to lie down. Off in the distance he could see the first deputy getting out of his car, putting on his coat, and reloading his gun.

What now, Francis? he said to himself. What now? They're going to shoot you whichever way you turn; they're going to kill you.

The aspen forest came up almost to the water's edge and there were patches of snow here and there. When he stood to run into the woods, he heard another snap, another sting, and fell and rolled down the slope. He was covered in leaves and dirt and came to a lean-to for animals. There was just enough room for him to squeeze under the shed from the back. And when his breathing slowed, he had a hard time staying awake.

In the dream that came on, the bear was there sniffing his face and pawing him without scratching. He put his hand out and felt the prickly fur. The bear stunk like he'd been rolling in shit, growled, and stretched out next to him, told him he would wait.

Wait for what? Francis said.

"I'll just wait," he said.

Part 2

Chapter 7

Dr. Glass: Where would you like to begin, Francis? Do you mind if I call you Francis? Where would you like to start our session today? I read your information, your history, so I know a little about you, and I read your brief statement. We can take care of the headache meds, too, before you leave. Would you prefer Francis or Frank?

Francis, and I think I'd like to start with the train? This is my first real time in counseling, except in the group home. So I'm not even sure what to say or where to begin. I saw the sign and came in. And I've got a pretty good idea why my headaches have come back, but I've just been dealing with them as best I can, lots of ibuprofen, and weed.

Dr. Glass: Self-medicating. Well, let's begin with the train and then you can connect it to your issue, why you've come to the clinic today, and somewhere along the way we can do a better job of introducing ourselves. So, please, tell me about the train. And hopefully we can get the headaches under control pretty quickly.

That's where Pindar lived.

Dr. Glass: Pindar lived on the train? And who is Pindar?

No, well, to the last stop, I rode the number 15 bus. That was before the train, while I was still in Denver.

Dr. Glass: You rode the 15 which was before the train? And what happened to Pindar?

Pindar lived at the ranch, near the train. He lived outside Doveless, east of Denver.

Dr. Glass: And Pindar was the ranch manager, one of the workers? Did you work there? Was there some kind of issue between you?

There was an issue, a big issue, but I got on the train after I got off the bus.

Dr. Glass: That's where you met Pindar, at the ranch by the train?

When the train slowed down, when it felt like it got slower, I jumped off.

Dr. Glass: And Pindar somehow was there, that's where you met him?

He was at the ranch, Pindar was there at the ranch that night, and I met him after I got off the train and walked on the road.

Dr. Glass: You didn't meet him on the road. He wasn't on the road?

Dr. Patel and the ambulance were there on the road. He saw me walking toward the ranch.

Dr. Glass: Wait, Pindar saw you walking on the road from the ambulance?

Dr. Patel saw me. He'd driven to the crossing, which is a whole other thing.

Dr. Glass: You're about to lose me. This Dr. Patel was waiting at the crossing, with the ambulance, not Pindar? And how did he know you were coming?

The whole other thing I mentioned, this is it. He would wait for them when the trains came, in case.

Dr. Glass: Ah, them. Now we're getting somewhere. In case what, and who is them?

Let me go back first. It was a great day on that train. It made a clicking sound, like music. I was on a flat-bed car, after the containers.

Dr. Glass: I'm having a hard time tracking. You were riding on a flat-bed car by the containers? And what about Pindar and Patel?

They came all the way from China.

Dr. Glass: That's a long way to come. And by they you mean Pindar and Patel or the containers, Francis.

Oh, sorry, I meant the containers came from China, not those two guys.

Dr. Glass: Wasn't it cold on the train? Did you have a good coat?

I did have a good coat. And there was a bear, too, a big brown-black bear.

Dr. Glass: You mean on the train with you? You saw it, spoke to it?

It was running alongside. Who knows where such a bear came from. But there he was.

Dr. Glass: The bear, was he in some way you, Francis? Or do you think this was a real bear?

He was real, as real as you and me. And regarding Patel, he waited for people, at the lights, that's where part of it started.

Dr. Glass: Dr. Patel waited for people like you coming from the train, walking along the road? And the "it" that got started seems pretty substantial. Can you say more about that?

He rigged up a problem at the crossing, so when they came, and the train was there, they got stuck.

Dr. Glass: Not sure what you're saying. Are you saying Dr. Patel caused a problem for people and the train and then there were collisions?

Not only were there collisions, but then he got their

organs. He was the one who trained me. That's what the ranch was all about, aside from being a regular ranch.

Dr. Glass: Maybe we should start over. I don't think I'm getting all this, especially about the organs. Let's begin at the beginning, shall we? Tell me about the train and the ranch, in order if you can. We have to watch the clock, too, for our session.

The Colfax bus, I took it all the way out from town, rode it all the way out. Where it stopped and people got off, at the end, on the second day, I could see a train, far away moving slow. Maybe I could catch it, I said. And I walked as fast as I could with my bag.

Dr. Glass: Did you have any idea where it might have been going, or did you care? And did you have something on your mind?

From the back I hopped on the caboose, then I moved up past the containers, to the flatbed, and there were box cars ahead all the way up to the engines. I stood near the box cars for a little shelter. The train picked up speed, and the wind came up. Cows in the field by the fences stopped to look. I didn't care where I was going.

Dr. Glass: Is this the same coat you were wearing, Francis, the one you have on now? I'm just wondering how you stayed warm. And were you at all frightened?

I lay down part of the time to rest, out of the wind, and looked up at the sky; it was blue-blue I remember that. And the bright sun, moving across. I didn't know where we would end up, Kansas maybe, Missouri. I wasn't too cold though. Sometimes when it made a little bit of a curve I could see the front and back at the same time. But I don't think they saw me.

Dr. Glass: It sounds beautiful. Did you enjoy riding the train? Seems like you did.

People waved. Kids in the back of a pick-up, motorcycles. The front engine blew the horn at the crossings, and the cars waited. It was a long train. I got hungry too, but I didn't have anything to eat.

Dr. Glass: Was there a reason why you took the train out there? Were you trying to get away from somebody or something?

Maybe there'll be a little store in a little town, I said, and then I can get off if it slows down. I didn't have much money, but maybe enough for a candy bar and something, a bottle of water. I liked the sound of the train a lot. There was no little store, though, and it didn't slow down, at least not right then; it picked up speed, it really got going, and I left because I helped Hennie, and then there was that guy.

Dr. Glass: Oh, you left Denver because of Hennie? And Hennie was your friend and something happened with another person, a guy? Were you depressed then? Am I accurate in saying you were depressed? But the meds are for your headaches, right, not the depression?

At the club I would clean up inside and around, the bathrooms, and the parking lot when it got dirty, it was all the work I could get. They didn't want me to drive the cars to park them; insurance, they said. And I worked at the front door too. Big Boy, that's what she called me. She was in charge of the girls. After a while they all called me that.

Dr. Glass: You mentioned a guy, Francis, in connection with Hennie; what did you want to say about that?

We were friends, Hennie and I. Can you do this for me, she would say, can you do that? Like errands. I was there only at night, it was good money, and they paid me in cash. I didn't want to work in the daytime because I was afraid they might find a reason to arrest me. But the girls were nice to me. And then there was that guy.

Dr. Glass: Something must have happened, Francis.

59

What happened? I noticed the two times you referred to him you looked down or out the window, and your face changed. Something must have happened. And you'll need to tell me why they wanted to arrest you, the police, I assume you mean.

Ten dollars, that's what my rent at the halfway house was, ten bucks a day. It was clean and they had showers. I'd been living under the bridge by the golf course before that. Sometimes I would see him there or at the Christian breakfast; there were other people living there too. And he would say things to me. Things about how tall I was, or how strange my face looked—how ugly, how I smelled. He wanted to see down below too, but I never did.

Dr. Glass: So you had trouble under the bridge, with another homeless man?

He liked to walk by the club, I would see him at night, on the sidewalk. He wanted to go in, I think, real bad, see the girls. Hennie told me to watch that guy, there's something strange about that guy, keep an eye on him. She came outside to smoke, around the side, and saw him one night. He was dressed up; he had a nice white shirt, a haircut; I didn't recognize him. But Hennie saw him. He's going to try to come in tonight, she said. Don't let him in.

Dr. Glass: And you stopped him; you didn't let him in? This was what, a men's club where you worked? Did you ever have issues with the women?

Closer and closer, he came. Walking back and forth across the parking lot and he looked like he was getting into the cars. I didn't leave the door at first. He called out to me, Injun, Mexican, monster, what the hell are you? Queer? I'm opening the door to Hennie's car. I'm getting into Hennie's car. I couldn't let him do that. Hennie was my friend.

Dr. Glass: You felt you had to help your friend so you left the door unguarded, didn't you, Francis? You were going to stop him.

He kept talking and talking, saying things, calling out, and I got down on my belly and looked under the cars. His feet and knees, I could see them. He was smoking marijuana. It was easy to smell, and he was laughing loud like a little kid. He never saw me or heard me. But I didn't have a choice. He was . . . I had to stop him.

Dr. Glass: Did you fight? Did you injure him, Francis? Did you hurt him or did he hurt you?

I never got a chance to say goodbye to Hennie. I didn't get my money that night either. I had to leave right away. The police came when somebody found him. His white shirt, his shirt was . . . messed up.

Dr. Glass: All right, so I'm hearing you say something pretty serious happened between you, and you ended up having to leave? I'd like to hear more about the guy you had all that trouble with, maybe what it meant for you.

The whole night I walked on Colfax. People called out to me, and the girls asked me if I wanted to go. Go where? I said. Ha-ha, they said. Missionary people handed out bus coupons. They gave me a coat. The moon was full, nearly full. And I walked a long time.

Dr. Glass: Francis, were you able to sleep, did you find some place to sleep?

A guy said he would give me twenty dollars to watch his black car. He gave me five to start and I got something to eat with that money. A bean and cheese burrito, two burritos because they were closing, one for free. They spoke Spanish to me. When I couldn't speak Spanish, they got mad. I was tired and found a shed in the rear of an apartment house. It had a few tools in it and a mower. With the doors shut I was ok, pretty warm. Nobody came around.

Dr. Glass: In the morning did you get back on the bus?

People were walking for exercise at the mall, and the coffee stand, they handed out samples of a sweet drink. It tasted like pumpkins and I drank as many as I could. The bus stopped there, but the walkers, with their cups, when I sat down they moved away. And security came and spoke to me, asked to see my I.D. Asked me about the blood on my shirt.

Dr. Glass: And where did you get the blood? Was this from that fellow at the club? This is beginning to sound much more serious.

I was only on the bus for a little while after the mall, and that's when I saw the train on the side, beyond the field and the road. The driver told everyone to get off, that was where the bus turned around. There was a fence, and I tore my coat on the wire, walking to the train, and later I had to get a patch. The more I hurried the farther away it seemed to get. At first I got on the caboose, but the door was locked, I tried to get in. Then the containers, the flat bed, and a box car, but I didn't want them to close the doors. So I stayed out, but next to the box cars.

Dr. Glass: Did you have this coat on, Francis, the one you're wearing? It looks pretty substantial.

How far the train was going, I didn't really know, but I rode it for a few hours, maybe two, until it started to slow down, it got sidetracked, there was another train going the other way.

Dr. Glass: Did you ever see the bear again, Francis? Was he there while you were riding?

He was running next to us and then behind, even when the train was going faster, I could see him. He could really run.

Dr. Glass: What color was he?

Dark brown, more black-brown.

Dr. Glass: And when the train finally did slow down?

He stopped and watched, stayed back. But he was there all the time; and the whole time I was at the ranch he was somewhere.

Dr. Glass: Was the other train a passenger train or freight train? And either way were there people on board?

Only freight trains run out there. I held onto the handle and got ready to jump down. My train was going faster than it looked; it was going too fast. I tried to keep up. Then I hit something, a sign, I didn't see it. Dr. Patel came when I tried to stand up, after the train had passed, and it seemed like he'd been there watching. There was blood on my face and in my hair. He unbuttoned my shirt before I knew what he was doing, put his hand on my heart; he was checking to see if I could be ready. And he put his finger in the blood on my head.

Dr. Glass: Whatever you tell me is private, Francis, and you don't have to tell me, but I'd like you to share with me, at least at some point, about the club, about what happened there, the violence. It would be a significant part of your treatment. Do you understand what I'm saying? So you hit something, a sign, and you were bleeding? Did you have a concussion?

Dr. Patel asked me what my blood type was, and called me cowboy. What is your blood type, cowboy? I didn't know, I told him. What are the types, I asked, but I knew. I'd been asked before, plenty of times, and had my blood drawn more than a couple times. They often wanted to do it again, to make sure, but I always said no.

Dr. Patel said, "I am Dr. Raj Patel. How is your head? That is a big cut and will definitely require stitches."

Dr. Glass: It seems so strange that he would put his hand inside your shirt to check your heart.

It was strange, but the whole deal was strange. So, Dr. Patel went back and brought his big first-aid kit. Then he cleaned my head real good and gave me a wet cloth to wipe my face and hair. Above my right eye, straight back, at the hairline, maybe twelve stitches, while I was sitting there. But

I've had a ton of them in the past. On my face and head, my arms and hands, so it wasn't that big of deal.

Dr. Glass: But I wonder what all those stitches mean, do you know what I'm saying?

Dr. Patel asked why I'd had so many stitches too. It's a psychology question, I think.

Dr. Glass: And what did you say to Dr. Patel?

I asked him why he was there at the train.

"In case there are accidents," he said, "and to help people who jump off."

Do lots of people jump off the train here? I asked.

"You would be surprised."

My head, I said, how bad? I've got a big headache.

"You should be all right; I will give you some ibuprofen, but it will not be pretty."

What's out here? I asked. What's here?

"Are you just now looking for a job?" he said wagging his head.

I guess so, I said, because I don't have much money.

"What is your name?" he said.

After a minute I said, Francis.

"Francis, do you have a family name?"

Francis for now.

Dr. Glass: Are you reluctant to share that part of your identity with people? That connection?

Mostly they automatically think the worst. Or they make a joke.

Dr. Glass: Then what happened with this Dr. Patel?

"Can you work?" he asked me. "You are big enough. But can you do hard work on a ranch? Pindar is always looking. And we have a transplant clinic."

That was the first time I'd heard his name and any mention of the clinic. I told Dr. Patel I could work. Did they have food and a place to stay?

"We have a bunkhouse," he said, "and all you can eat."

How do they pay?

"Every week for ranch work," he said, "more for the operating room, for the transplants."

What operating room? I asked. What is that?

"Ever worked in a hospital?"

Veterinary, I said. I helped a veterinarian for one summer, in high school.

"Can you learn or are you just a big fellow?"

I said it depended on what it was. Some things, like bussing tables, I'm pretty slow at.

"Do you want to ride with me back to the ranch, meet Pindar, make your decision?"

Dr. Patel was driving the ambulance and when I looked up the sky had turned gray.

How far? I asked.

"Four miles," he said.

I think I'll just walk, I said. I didn't know what to make of Dr. Patel or the ranch.

Dr. Glass: Francis, where exactly is this place, I have no idea?

It's way the hell out there. Before Anton, above Limon, near the town of Doveless.

Dr. Glass: I don't think I've ever been out that way. And what did Patel say when you said you wanted to walk? Maybe that was your intuitive side at work.

He said, "Ok, go to the new red building when you get there. And Pindar will want to know about your blood." Then he drove away, but slow and watched me in the mirror.

Not sure why but I had the feeling they could see me; they were looking at me the whole way. The road was a good dirt road, and there were lots of little cows behind the fences. The wire was electric. But they came to look at me, and thought I might have feed.

When I needed to take a leak I stepped over the electric fence and went into the trees. There were bones on the ground and a hide, a small stream, cottonwoods and aspen. It started to rain-snow, the little pellets.

Dr. Glass: Graupel.

What does that mean, graupel?

Dr. Glass: The rain-snow, it's called graupel, from the German.

A flock of blackbirds flew up from the top of the trees, shifted left and right, the whole group. I thought I heard them whistling. Then they disappeared. The tall grass was blowing over from the wind, the heads. I didn't want to leave the trees. I didn't know what was coming at the ranch, but it was getting colder. I was all right, aside from the headache, but thought maybe I wouldn't go to the house, I'd get back on another train. So I began walking toward the crossing. But before I'd walked very far, I stopped. What is there for you in Denver? I said out loud. What is there? Only more shit. I could see the ranch in the distance, the lights and the buildings, lots of lights. One night, two nights, I said to myself, and then leave if you don't like it; you can always leave. There was an airport on the right as I walked on the road, little but wide and long, with a windsleeve for the wind.

Dr. Glass: A windsleeve? I wonder what they were doing with an airport? Right about now you were probably thinking that that place was pretty weird.

I was, yeah, and there were planes inside their garages, even a jet. As I got closer to the red building I could see a man outside standing in the German graupel. He was wearing an oxygen mask, and had a light shirt on, like for summer, with a small belly. The wind was blowing his hair, he was holding it and it was all white, thin. I couldn't tell if he was an old man or just a man who looked old. He didn't wave or move until I got close, right up to him.

Dr. Glass: That's a long way from the club to the ranch in one day, totally different worlds. That must've seemed strange.

"Francis," he said, and shook my hand with both of his. "I'm Pindar, this is my place. Dr. Patel informed me you were on the train and would be walking, and that maybe you were interested in a ranch job."

Here I am, I said to myself, I'm here at this ranch. What should I do?

"You're a pretty good-sized fella," he said. "You're what, six-eight, six-nine, with a mean-looking cut on your head?"

With the wind and his oxygen mask, I could barely hear him talking, and he went on. It sounded like a mumbled whisper, only a little louder. His eyes moved like the birds that shifted. Left and right, left and right.

Yes, I said, to whatever I thought he said, maybe the six-eight or six-nine question or the job question. But I was watching the whole time.

"Ah," he said after a minute of looking at me with loud mumbling, "and you do look like you might make a pretty good ranch man, but have you ever worked in a clinic or hospital?"

"I did neutering, large animals, in a veterinary hospital once."

"Well," he said laughing, "maybe there's something there that'd apply. We do very high-end surgery, organ transplants, privatized. Know anything about that?"

Nothing, I said, only what I've seen on TV. But then I said to myself, What the hell are you talking about?

Actually, at first I thought I heard him say Oregon transplants, private eyes.

Dr. Glass: With a mask on I could see how you'd think that, and wonder just what was going on, big time.

"Dr. Patel might be looking for someone to train one of

67

these days," Pindar said. "We'll talk. What I've started here at the ranch is all very revolutionary. No one is doing anything remotely similar anywhere in the world. In five years I'll be known as the Barnard of the private transplant industry. And which part did you mean yes to? The job or your height?"

We were standing on the porch; there were fancy cactus plants, plants with big needles in pots growing all around. I could see Pindar was starting to shiver, he was shaking, and I wanted to make him stay out. But I didn't say anything back about the job or my height.

Dr. Glass: Why did you want him to stay out in the cold?

Not sure, I just, I don't know, maybe wanted to test him, see how he handled it.

"What's your blood type?" he finally said. "Know what your blood type is?"

What are the different types? What kinds are there? I said.

"Let's get your blood checked and then we can do a backgrounder on you, make sure you're not a convicted murderer. If everything's ok, you can start in the morning on the ranch. We get up early here, at five. You ok with that?"

I said I was, that I'd be ready, and did they have a pair of gloves I could borrow, that they could loan me?

"We got plenty of gloves, Tallman. Many as you need. We'll get you introduced and then you can find a place to sleep in the bunkhouse. Somethin' about you, Tallman. Not sure what it is, but something. You're not a smoker are you? That's strictly forbidden anywhere on the ranch."

No, I said, not a smoker. Never smoked.

"Even dope?" he asked.

Even dope, I said, though I smoke if someone offers, but I never buy it.

We looked at each other for a minute, stared.

"Nice coat," he finally said.

And I looked down, looked at my torn coat that was too

tight. I thought he was making a joke, he was trying to be funny, so I ignored him.

"All right then," Pindar said, "all right."

And he picked up his oxygen, looked at me again, and we went inside.

8.

Dr. Glass: Are you ready? Should we start? How have you been this week, Francis? Would you like a bottle of water? And if you have any questions about me, my background, my education, feel free to ask. We haven't had our proper introduction. We sort of skipped that last week. Like you, though, I'm pretty new to the Indigent Program. This is my first time too. How's your head doing?

Oh, I always have a little bit of a headache, but it's ok.

Dr. Glass: Maybe we can pick up from last week. I think we were talking about Mr. Pindar and your first meeting.

Yeah, on the ranch they kept asking about my blood, they always wanted to know, Pindar did, but I hate needles. I didn't want them to check. At first I couldn't figure out what the deal was.

Dr. Glass: They wanted to know what? Do you mean your blood type? Why in the world? Are you a little phobic about giving blood? Have you had this fear for a long time? So what do you think of when you see a needle?

When I was growing up it seemed like the adults were always trying to test me. It wasn't that it hurt so much, but I just didn't like the sticking, and the attention.

Dr. Glass: Francis, do you have a special kind of blood? Are you AB-negative or something like that?

You see the Great Grandfather comes from Geneva and Ingolstadt. We've traced him, the oldest Grandfather, to around 1750. Before that, we couldn't find anybody. It was like he hadn't existed. But the Doctor was the key; he was the one.

Dr. Glass: And is that a Swiss name, Stein? Are your parents Germanic, or Jewish?

That's the shortened form. When my father came here he changed it. At the ranch they had a good time, the other guys, Beattie mostly, with Stein.

Dr. Glass: I'm interested in hearing more about the Doctor and your family, but I'm really curious about this ranch. Before we go there, though, I'd like to ask again about the club and about the fellow who was by the cars, by Hennie's car. Are you ready to talk about that?

Right away on the first day we had to pull the shingles off the barn. They were wood, and because I was new, I had to carry all the replacement bundles up the ladder. I didn't mind because it was a big barn, three stories, and I could see all over the country. Down south, up north. It took us three days of hard work. And Pindar watched from a chair with his oxygen, and that noisy breathing. That was the start with Beatty too.

Dr. Glass: So many new names. Beatty is who?

It started right there on the roof. Beatty was the one nailing most of the shingles. He was good-sized and he liked to cuss. The rest of us were the helpers. We did all the hauling and hammering the old nails in, cutting the decking, rolling out the felt. And every day it was hard work on the ranch; every day something different. Then when we were done with the barn it was time to move the cows around. We had to move them to new pastures, more than 500, maybe as many as 800. We took care of their water, too, broke up the ice, fed them hay, made sure they were ok. Sometimes the calves weren't ok. But I liked the work. Four of us, including Beatty, and a bunch of part-timers.

We drove around in pick-ups, two of us, with all the tools we needed for the day. We would be out morning till night sometimes. We had to take our lunches.

Dr. Glass: How big was the ranch, Francis, do you remember? Can you describe it? And sounds like you liked it out there.

It was pretty big. One day we were over near the crossing, I could see it down below, and I watched to find out if any people jumped off, like Dr. Patel said, and a train had just passed by. But no one was there, no one got off. I was also looking to find out if a car came by what would happen with whatever Dr. Patel did to the tracks. No cars or trucks came while we were there, and then we had to leave. It took us a long time to drive there, and then a while to get to the next job, which was by the creek.

The water at the creek was frozen, mostly frozen but not too thick. There were a few ducks on the edge, in the reeds. And a little dam, with a pool behind; it was kind of plugged up; we had to clean it out to let the water flow. We cleaned it out with our hands and the water was so cold.

We saw a coyote, too, and he stopped to watch us, then ran away. Epiphanio, that was the other guy, the guy driving, little Epiphanio from Mexico, said he must have a house somewhere nearby because he'd seen that same one before. Most of the days it was sunny, no clouds, with some wind in the afternoon, and some snow. I liked being on the ranch those days; I liked it a lot, even with Beatty.

Dr. Glass: I'm curious now about this Beatty. Can we go back to him? Sounds like he was an antagonistic character. Have you had to tangle with these kinds of people before?

As an example he liked to call me Sasquatch, and then do things like throw my boots outside. That's the kind of person he was. He was smaller than me, maybe six-two, but he had shoulders. He knew how to work.

At dinner Beatty made sure he was first in line, every time, and in the bunkhouse, he had his radio loud, he wouldn't turn it off, all night. Heavy metal. Pindar never said anything. Beatty would say, "You got a problem" and then curse. Like, "You got a problem with that, fucking asshole?" The other two never said anything. They were small, both from Mexico. So he came after me. I like to read Westerns at night. But he wouldn't let me. He didn't want me to read. He wanted to wrestle and fight in the bunkhouse. I didn't want to fight him. I knew what would happen.

"Pindar called you Tallman," Beatty said. "but you look like a ugly-ass girl to me, with a rock for a head."

He would get into my stuff. I didn't have much, but he would get into my things. I had an old rosary that I found, and a picture of Hennie in an outfit. And he took them. He held up the picture and said he wanted to fuck Hennie and he put the rosary around his neck and then in his pants. I kept trying to read, tried hard to read, but I knew something was going to happen.

When it did he went after Epiphanio first and dragged him out of his bed. He knew that I would do something, that I would say something.

Stop that, Beatty, I said. Let him alone.

"Is that the rockhead talking now," he said. "The tall girl with the sewed-up brain?"

Dr. Glass: You must have been frightened, Francis. I would have been. The classic profile of a bully.

As soon as he touched me I knocked him down. I didn't want to hurt him; I didn't want Pindar to say anything. I wanted him to be able to work. But he kept fighting and finally I bent his arm in the back until his bones cracked, until he quit.

Dr. Glass: That sounds pretty serious.

"Hey," he said while he was still on the floor breathing hard, "I was just messing with you, man, just having some fun. Not sure I can move my arm."

In the morning, Pindar asked if something happened, if something went on in the bunkhouse. I let Beatty answer and he said he went to bed early; he didn't remember anything happening. And Beatty had a hard time working that day.

Pindar assigned us to the same truck in the morning, and right away Beatty got out his meth pipe, started talking real loud. The cows had knocked down a fence, they'd busted the electric fence down somehow, and we had to go get them, fix the fence. It took us a while to get there, and I had the window down all the way. When Beatty was high he talked about his ex-wife, his kids, he had three kids somewhere, and that he was going to take one of the trucks and leave the ranch.

These were yearlings, black and red angus, and they couldn't decide what to do when they saw us. Beatty knew enough to swing around, partially block the ones that were out with the truck. We got most of them back in the pasture, we herded them back, and with a stick I went to get two that thought they might want to escape. Soon as I got far enough away from the truck and where he was, Beatty started it up and left me behind, drove off laughing, beeping the horn, which scared the cows.

Dr. Glass: He just left you, this Beatty? Were you worried that you'd be stuck out there or something would happen? I would have been. A classic aggressive-dominance relationship.

I got the two cows inside the fence, made certain the electricity was back on, then looked around to be sure Beatty wasn't hiding somewhere, and started walking. Didn't have much choice. It was just before noon, maybe eleven-thirty, and I had eight or ten miles to go, so I knew it wouldn't be dark before I got back.

And about being worried, I wasn't too nervous, but what I noticed when I was out there walking was how quiet it was. I could hear myself walking, my footsteps, right foot, left foot. And before that I never noticed that I dragged my right foot a little bit, but I do. And there were little plants that I hadn't ever seen before. One of them looked like a TV antenna, a Martian TV antenna, the way it poked out to receive messages.

Dr. Glass: Despite the distance, I hear you saying it was a real nature encounter.

It was to start. Halfway or so, there was a bluff, and down below there was a little bridge, a small bridge over the creek. From the bluff, up top, I could see Beatty's truck had driven off the bridge and overturned. The creek was dry right there and there wasn't any water, but the truck was upside down. First thing I did when I got there was hurry over and make sure to feel his pulse. It looked like he'd broken his neck. There was still a little heartbeat, not much, but something. The second thing, after seeing if he had a pulse, was look around for that pipe and the meth, I knew he had it, and throw both away. When I found them I tossed them as far as I could so no one would find them.

Dr. Glass: An interesting turn of events. How long had he been there? What did you do? And I'll be interested to know how you felt.

He'd probably been there forty or fifty minutes. When I tried the doors they wouldn't open, I didn't know what to do, so I pulled him out the passenger window, squeezed him out head first. It took a little bit to get him to the road. Then I had to get him on my shoulders, and he was heavy, real heavy. I had to drape his arms.

But walking ten feet with a heavy dead man, let alone

five miles, and one you don't like that much, is a lot more than hard. It's nearly impossible. As I started to climb up the road on the other bank with Beatty, I remembered he had a cell phone, I'd heard him use it, and I set him down. It was in his coat pocket and in his address book was Pindar's phone.

"Beatty," Pindar said when I called the number, "what's up out there? You and Lurch get those cows back?"

Pindar, I said, it's Francis. Beatty's dead. He overturned the truck on the creek; drove off the bridge and broke his neck.

"Fucking guy was probably smoking that crack again. How long?"

Not too long, maybe less than an hour.

"Where is he?"

I pulled him out of the truck. He's right here. I'm carrying him on the road.

"What the hell were you going to do, carry him back to the house?"

Yeah, I said, I didn't know what else to do.

"Francis, we'll be there in five minutes with the ambulance. Just wait."

Holding him up, with my arms around him and looking at his face, I said, Beatty, Beatty, you made a mess of things, turned the truck over, killed yourself. Now your kids got no father at all. What are you going to do? Off a-ways, I could hear the ambulance speeding over the road, and before long I knew they would take him away. I didn't expect an answer, of course, I didn't expect him to say anything to me, but I wondered what he might've said if he could talk, if he wasn't dead. But if he wasn't dead he wouldn't have wanted to talk to me anyway.

It seemed like only a second had passed before Pindar was there, and Dr. Patel and the Mexicans held him up and cut his clothes off before they put him in the ambulance. Inside they swabbed him down with antiseptic twice, head to foot, but especially around his heart. They told me to drive and Pindar sat in the passenger side with his respirator. Dr. Patel and the Mexicans continued to clean him with swabs and trim his hair off. They were wearing white, not blue like on TV.

What's going to happen? I asked Pindar. What are you doing?

Dr. Glass: I'm pretty curious, too. What did happen?

"The recipient has been notified," Pindar said. "Our jet will pick him up in an hour. Beatty's heart will be in a new body before morning."

You're going to do a heart transplant right here? I asked. On the ranch?

"In our state-of-the-art operating room," he said. "You can watch from the gallery, unless Dr. Patel needs you."

They continued to listen to his heart, to watch it on a screen, to see if it was beating and somewhere along the way, I could see in the mirror, it stopped completely.

Dr. Glass: Wait, wait. They did transplants on this ranch? You mean like the major organs?

Yes, including hearts.

Dr. Glass: Wow, it's an understatement to say a lot happened on the ranch that day, Francis. Beatty drove off and left you. You walked back and found him, carried him. They brought the ambulance and put him inside. They got him ready for a heart transplant. But the whole thought of them doing transplants so casually is unbelievable, really disturbing. And out on a ranch.

That's what I thought when they first said it. It's true, though, and that afternoon Dr. Patel told me to stay close, get cleaned up and change, that they might need my help in the operating room. But none of the medical clothes fit me, so I had to wear everything too short. At first it seemed like they were kidding about the transplants.

Dr. Glass: I have so many questions about this whole organization. And I'm extremely curious about the operating room, whether it was well equipped, what it looked like, how big, and how antiseptic it was. What with sepsis and all that. Nowhere in the literature have I heard of something like this happening. The fact that it was even out there. And here's another question: Did they ever get a release from Beatty, some kind of donor-pledge program when he was hired?

Pindar was sitting in the gallery reading the newspaper when he got the call. The recipient was on his way, the guy who needed the heart was coming. They had to take Beatty's heart out of his chest and put it on ice. When I saw him lying there he was naked, stretched out, and some of the tools they were going to use made me want to leave, and I turned to go out. No, no, Dr. Patel said, you will be staying here. It was real cold in the operating room, but Beatty probably didn't mind, and before you know it, Epiphanio and the other Mexican, Javier, had everything in place and there was a big timer counting down—14:11, 9:27, 4:43, :00.

Dr. Glass: And did they have the very latest equipment? That's another thing. Or was it primitive and recycled?

They said they had the latest equipment, but I wouldn't know. Did I say there was music? There was music playing, but not too loud.

Dr. Glass: What kind of music? Did you like it? I can't exactly tell how you felt then.

It was piano orchestra music. I didn't like it. And I felt like I was in a weird kind of circus or carnival.

"Stand behind the line," Dr. Patel said pointing when we began, "unless I call you. Everything will go very fast. Listen to my voice, watch my movements."

One last time Dr. Patel smoothed his hand over Beatty, then they cut his chest open with a knife, then a saw, a little power saw, and had these things to spread his bones, pry his chest open and keep it open. When Patel looked a certain way or turned, Epiphanio or Javier had whatever he needed right there. No pause or questions. Then Dr. Patel stood there looking down for a moment.

"Was Beatty using drugs when he died?" he called out to me.

Yes, I said, he was.

"Solution," he said to Epiphanio, and he sprayed a clear liquid on the heart. He repeated, blotted it up, and then waited. "Superior vena cava," he called out and then cut something at the top of the heart with a surgical knife Javier handed him. "Aorta," he said, and cut three times. "Pulmonary artery, pulmonary vein." He continued to cut and call out names. "Left coronary artery, circumflex artery." Then when he was finished, he backed away and raised his hands. The two Mexicans lifted the heart and set it in a container on an ice pack and covered it.

"We are ready," Dr. Patel said. "Too bad we did not have a use for the other organs if Beatty was a healthy man, and there were recipients, which we will see about."

Dr. Patel was upset over something, I could see, but he went about his business.

"Listen for it," Pindar said pointing at the ceiling and holding his watch. "Should be circling any second."

And a half minute later we heard an airplane pass over, a jet from the airport. Dr. Patel told me to go with Epiphanio and Javier, to help them, and to drive the ambulance to the airport. While I drove, the two of them scrubbed the rolling bed in the back.

Dr. Glass: You mean the gurney? That's what they're called.

The gurney and the walls and the floor, but when we pulled up to the jet, the guy who was getting the heart got off the plane, he walked off the plane on his own power, except for a cane. In the light I could see he had a kind of funny color, like he hadn't been outside much, gray-white and pale blue. As we rode along I could hear him talking to Epiphanio, asking scared questions, maybe because he was so afraid, and I thought that in just a few minutes, the heart that was laying in the operating room on ice would be his heart, it would be in his chest.

While I drove I wondered what they would do with Beatty. They had put a cloth over him, like a sheet, during the operation and there was a lot of blood everywhere. Would they put him on ice? Would they just wrap him up and set him out of the way? Or would they lay him on a pile of wood at the ranch and burn him up like they do in India?

When we stopped at the operating room and I went around the back of the ambulance, the guy put his hand on my shoulder and said, "You think it would be all right if I walked next to you? I'm a little nervous right now and you look pretty sturdy."

I put my arm around his waist, held him up, and we walked in together.

"Stay with me," he said when we got inside, "stay with me as long as you can." There were tears in his eyes and his hand was shaking on my shoulder. I stayed with him, helped him get out of his clothes. He sat there with nothing on except white slippers and he put his hands on his head. He was in pretty good shape, but, well, how to say it, he had breasts, like a woman, only smaller and saggy, a little belly, and his dick and balls hung way down.

"I don't know why I'm doing this," he said shaking his head. "Why am I doing this?"

Pindar opened the door of the recovery room, looked around for a second, then walked up to the man and shook his hand. He shook his hand and called his name. I can't remember what his name was, Lawrence maybe, and sat down next to him.

"This man is a captain of industry," Pindar said looking

at me. "A leader of the free world. Wealthy beyond imagination. He has it all. And he's here with us. No lists to get on. No bureaucratic approvals. Organ transplants - privatized. That might even be our name."

He didn't look like anybody I'd ever seen before; I'd never seen him in the newspaper or in magazines, even on TV.

"Who gives a shit about any of that stuff now, Pindar? I feel as weak and as vulnerable as the next man. More so because I'm used to being in charge. I'm not in charge right now. I'm helpless, goddamnit, and I'm about to get even more helpless."

The man burst out crying again and Pindar patted him on the back and walked out. Before he put on his gown he asked me to hold him, two men, for just a moment, and we stood there - him shivering, him naked next to me.

Dr. Patel came in and helped him tie up his gown, talked to him again about what was going to happen, the order of things, and what he could expect after, then helped him get onto the bed, the gurney.

"Is it all right if this fellow stays with me the whole time," he said to Dr. Patel, meaning me.

"Ah, Francis," he said pointing, "the newest member of our team, yes, that would be fine, of course, yes."

He had a strong grip, that man, and he didn't let go of my hand. He asked to see the new heart and they brought it to him. Then they began attaching different things to him, fluids and medicines, drainage, things like that. They set the timer again and gave the guy something to knock him out.

Before he was under completely, though, he called out for Pindar.

"Pindar," he said, "Pindar. Where the hell are you?"

"I'm here, Lawrence, I'm here. What is it?"

"I don't want to die, Pindar. I don't want to die. Do you understand me? Whatever it costs."

He had a hold of Pindar's shirt; I was on the other side gripping his hand, and then the medicine kicked in and he let go and collapsed onto the table. The countdown clock showed they were out of time and they began. Pindar looked at him lying there and told him he wasn't going to die.

It was a lot like Beatty's operation, except with Beatty he was dead; he was dead and they didn't have to worry about making any mistakes. I had to get out of the way, had to let go of his hand, and Patel pointed right where I should stand. The operating room had so many lights and machines going it was hard to see where I was supposed to be. Two heart operations in just a few hours, and I'd hardly ever been in a clinic or a hospital, except for my various stitches. But I had a hard time watching.

They had to clean him up real good like Beatty before everything began, I forgot to say that, and this time it seemed like they were rougher on him. He didn't have as much hair on his body as Beatty, but they still had to take some off. They took it off around his chest, down to his crotch, and washed him.

Dr. Glass: What size person was this man, the heart recipient, and did he remind you of anyone? While you were talking it looked like maybe you had some feelings about him.

He was kind of skinny, a strong kind of skinny, and he had small shoulders. He reminded me of a teacher, one of my teachers in high school, when I was still going, Mr. Seddle. When they had auto-shop. I don't know why he liked me, but he did. I was big then too, and he let me eat lunch in the shop when I didn't want to go outside, I helped out. I could fix things and I would ask him questions. Eventually Mr. Seddle had to go to the hospital himself and I went to see him, I found out where he was, and I visited him. The guy with the heart, Lawrence, he looked like Mr. Seddle, except Lawrence was much older. And when he started to cry while he was sitting naked, it almost made me want to cry. It was a sad kind of thing to see an old man there crying.

Dr. Glass: I'm still so overwhelmed with this whole thing and you going from being a cowboy one second to a transplant tech the next. And Francis, I'm real curious, how they even figured out that the fellow who crashed the truck, Beatty, had compatible blood. How they matched people up so quickly. Any idea about that? Depending on how long you were there, you probably learned all about their program.

They had a blood bank on the ranch. They said it was for the community, for Doveless and around that area. And they had blood drives, got people to sign organ-donor forms, including Beatty. Pindar told people it was for them, just in case of emergency operations or things like that. But it was more for his OTP, the organ transplants. From the beginning they wanted to know about my blood; they said they needed to know what everybody's blood type was and that everybody had to give blood to work there. I didn't want to, I never wanted to tell them or give blood. Nobody has my type of blood anyway, one in a million, so it's a waste. When they demanded I told them I quit, I didn't want to work there, and I left. This was after working for a month.

I started out walking on the road to the crossing. I was either going to hitchhike or hop on the train. Dr. Patel came in his car and rolled down the window next to me. He said I didn't have to give blood if I didn't want, it was ok. I said I was leaving anyway, I didn't like the ranch, that it was a strange place. We had performed three more transplants. He asked if I was interested in becoming a transplant technician, like Epiphanio and Javier. It was much better money. I said I'd think about it, but kept walking. He handed Beatty's phone out the window and told me it was mine now.

"Ok, Francis," he said, "call me if you need a ride. I will come get you."

At the crossing there was a bridge, a nice iron bridge, with graffiti and paint, and I climbed down underneath to wait for the train. I closed my eyes and dreamed; mostly about bloody hearts or seeing Beatty's face up close to mine when I carried him, or the guy at the club by the cars. And I heard cars crossing above, but no train. Then a car came, a red car with teenagers. Two boys. They had alcohol and a girl, and they wanted to wait until the train came to throw beer cans at it. I could hear every word from down below. I wanted to tell them not to drive onto the tracks when they heard the train, to leave so nothing happened.

But the boy driving, we had seen him before when we went into town with Pindar for the blood drive, he wanted to scare the other two. He wanted the girl to take off her clothes. He was laughing and drinking, and he locked the doors on the car so no one could get out. He drove up on the tracks and was going to drive off when the train got too close. But Patel's trap caught him; it caught all of them.

Dr. Glass: Stop a second. You mean that something that Dr. Patel did, a device of some kind prevented them from driving off the tracks?

It was a terrible sound, the sound of the train hitting the car, and the girl screaming.

Dr. Glass: What did you do, Francis? Did the train stop? Were the kids hurt or killed?

It took a long time for the train, the train couldn't stop right away. They're not like a pick-up truck. This one was all coal, very heavy. And the red car got smashed bad; it got knocked along the tracks, then off to the side. The girl and the boy in the back were killed; it killed them right away, and threw them out. But the boy behind the wheel was still alive. He was bleeding from his head and chest, but still alive. I talked to him. He begged me not to let him die, and to save the other two.

I called Dr. Patel and told him what happened. He asked me if the boy had a tag on his wrist, a white tag.

He does, I said.

"What does it show is his blood type and does it have a capital D?"

The tag said A-positive and it had a D.

"And the other two? What about them? Tags?"

I said I thought they were crushed, that they were pretty badly injured, and neither had tags.

"I will be there in a few minutes. Do not move the boy behind the wheel."

The other two were off to the side, and I put them together and carried them to the bridge. Then I went to the boy behind the wheel. He talked a little before he died, or he tried.

"My parents," he said with big gaps, "they're gonna be. . . ."

His breaths had a gurgly sound. I put my hand on his shoulder.

" . . . and those two kids . . . I never meant to. . . ."

By then the two train guys were there. They had a first-aid kit.

"Those kids were stuck," one of them said. "Looked like they got stuck on something on the track. We saw 'em but couldn't get it stopped."

Then Dr. Patel and Epiphanio, Javier, were there and they loaded all three.

"How long since this boy has been gone," Dr. Patel asked me.

Just a few minutes, I said, but I'm not sure, better check to see if he's gone.

They checked the other two and decided they were too badly injured. Their heads were wide open from where they'd hit, like in the movies, and they had big gashes in their chests and bellies and things were hanging out. There was blood all over my clothes from where I'd carried them.

Dr. Glass: That's a horrific story and I wouldn't doubt if you're suffering from PTSD. So what did you do, Francis? Get on the train or go back with them?

I drove the ambulance. I wasn't sure what to do, so that day I drove the ambulance.

9.

Dr. Glass: How've you been this week, Francis? Still have the security job? I think you were worried about that, weren't you? And you're still living at the same place, in the basement? That was a terrible story we had to leave on, those three kids. We should check in about your headaches, too, if we have time. You know, I'm really interested in finding out whether that man, Lawrence. . . .

I've been thinking about the bear today. He came to the bunkhouse some nights when the lights were out; he was around the ranch, and scratched at the windows. I don't know where he lived, but I thought at first he was sleeping down below something, a shed or an outbuilding, maybe he dug a hole under somewhere.

Dr. Glass: He wasn't hibernating in a cave? You mean you don't think he slept outside somewhere?

On the prairie it's not so easy to sleep outside. And after a while I figured it was him who was knocking the fences down, letting the cows out. Bears can be funny like that. And they're not so afraid of electricity, which I understand. I asked Epiphanio and Javier if they ever saw the bear, if they ever heard him. *Que hoso*, they said. Pindar and Dr. Patel too. Nobody saw or heard him but me.

Dr. Glass: Is it possible that it was the bushes scratching

against the window and a coyote knocking the fences down? Or could it have been, maybe, from a dream? I think bears frequently appear as representations of men in dreams and certainly in mythology.

The man you asked about, Lawrence, was ok for a while, for a few days, a week probably, they were ready to take the tubes and IVs out, he was up walking, then something happened. Dr. Patel called it post-operative stress and organ rejection. He'd been taking the medicine to prevent it though. But I knew what the problem was with Lawrence, I knew what it was right away.

Dr. Glass: What was the problem, Francis? Do you think they made a mistake of some kind?

When I was there with him afterward, helping him, I could see he was trying to cover up, not right away but pretty soon, he was trying not to show he was in pain. He didn't want there to be a problem. It hurt him all over his new heart. Then one day he coughed hard, he had a coughing fit, and the blood came, a little at first in his shit, then from his nose and mouth, there was a leak somewhere.

Dr. Glass: So Dr. Patel didn't tie something off or sew something together right? And did they open him back up?

It was Beatty's heart. It wasn't Dr. Patel. Once he started to put it in he couldn't stop. It was the drugs Beatty took, the crack. The heart was too weak; it was too soft, the veins and arteries, and it was too soon after he'd had the drugs.

Dr. Glass: But shouldn't Dr. Patel have known that, recognized that the heart was compromised?

It was Lawrence, too. He paid Pindar extra money, a lot of extra money, and he was ready, he was at the top of the private list. He couldn't wait, he didn't want to wait for the regular outside list, and he was getting sicker every day. So when Beatty had the accident, there was a match, they were both on Pindar's list, and Lawrence was willing to take a chance. They sent the jet as soon as they knew.

Dr. Glass: Any idea how much it cost to be on Pindar's list?

Not cheap, I know that. The boy at the bridge was the one we saw in town when we went there, the night Pindar took us all there for hamburgers. The boy behind the wheel. He was on the football team, maybe the captain, and we saw him in the game after we ate. The other two were there on the sidelines.

Dr. Glass: Oh, this is the boy whose car was hit by the train? The one with the two friends?

The boy was strong and he was older, a little bit older. But he was still in high school.

Dr. Glass: They didn't call his parents to tell them what they were going to do?

Here's the thing: Dr. Patel and Epiphanio and Javier got him ready. He had a good heart, but a weird kind of thing happened. I don't think he was dead; he wasn't quite dead, or it didn't seem like it. He didn't register on the machines, but because he was strong, somehow he just came back, he came back to life. That boy was alive when they cut his chest open, and I could see his mouth and eyes, they were both big, big as the moon, and maybe I thought I heard him say no, no, no, with tears in his eyes, or maybe I didn't, and Pindar yelled for them to continue, and Dr. Patel did continue. He continued and took his heart out and put it in another man's chest and that man lived and he's walking around today with a live heart, one from a live person, not a dead person, like the way they do it normally. But it really did a number on me. One of the many things.

Dr. Glass: I can understand that, and I don't know what to say. It's so hard to believe they took a live person's heart out, a boy's, and that they didn't see him. It's just too disturbing. And also that he might've been trying to say something, and that he might've been alive. It almost makes me sick. I completely understand why it bothered you so much.

His parents came as soon as Pindar called, they came as soon as they could; they lived on the other side of the county, but Pindar told them that the boy had signed the form. He said he'd signed the form and he was eighteen, and they took his heart out. His mother broke down.

Dr. Glass: And you were right there the whole time, from the beginning? All these events happening one after the other.

At night I hear the train-horn and the car, and I hear the sound of the girl screaming, the boy talking to me, telling me not to let him die, but I let him die, and maybe he could've lived.

Dr. Glass: Francis, it wasn't your fault. What could you do? But I can't imagine being his parents and learning that their son was dead, and not only dead but his heart had been cut out of his chest and was there waiting to be put into some-one else's chest who'd paid an exorbitant amount of money.

Beatty had lots of sayings or jokes before he died in the accident. Ones about the cows and how beautiful they were beginning to look, about not having any women at night, and he always liked to say the money flows when the jet goes.

Dr. Glass: I'm still pretty curious about this strange ranch, and the operating room. Was it clean, was it sanitary, was it spotless? I mean, there could have been big problems if the operating room was the least bit unclean. Not to mention your hands, your hair, your clothes.

Somewhere, like the East Coast or for rich people, Dr. Patel was well known, he was pretty well known for his operations, he'd done over a hundred, he said. And some-thing happened, maybe he had a problem, maybe he made a mistake, and Pindar contacted him and he came to work at the ranch, but on commission. When he came he trained Epiphanio and Javier, Beatty, in how to assist him. Beatty was clumsy but not the Mexicans. Plus, he showed them how to keep the operating room clean. How to make it very clean all the time. He was a good teacher in that way.

Dr. Glass: Did you get trained as a transplant technician and how to sterilize everything, the walls, the different kinds of equipment?

Yes, Patel trained me to do everything. Anyway, about Lawrence, Pindar liked to have fires outside at night. He liked having a bonfire and telling stories, roasting wieners. And he liked for us to sing.

Dr. Glass: What songs did he like you to sing? But I'd like to hear more about the operating room.

Pindar liked old songs, he liked us to sing country songs and old songs. *Freight train, freight train goin' so fast, freight train, freight train goin' so fast. Please don't tell what train I'm on, so they won't know where I'm gone.*

Dr. Glass: You have a good voice, Francis. Sing another stanza or another song.

One night Lawrence came out. He had his IV stand and he stood by the fire. He tried to sing but he couldn't. He couldn't sing because his voice was raspy due to the tubes, the ones he'd had in his throat. He sat in Pindar's chair. This was right before he got sick and died. He shouldn't have been outside, but Dr. Patel said it was ok. He was standing inside watching us at first. Pindar gave him a torch and he held it up. He held it up and we cheered him like he was the Olympic champion. But he looked like he was going to catch himself on fire with the torch. He was weak and shaky and nearly dropped it.

When he went back inside, Pindar said he wanted to show us something. He wanted to take us for a ride, but not Lawrence. So we all climbed into one pick-up. Patel drove and Pindar was in the passenger seat. Me and Epiphanio and Javier, the three of us, were in the back with horse blankets. We drove a long way, over one hill then another, crossed a bridge, then parked.

"Do you see that?" Pindar asked when we were all standing outside on one of the hills. I watched him breathing and that combined with the night wind, and his talking, I thought we were in a sci-fi scene and that the aliens would be dropping in any minute.

What he was talking about was lights for what looked like a little town, maybe a half mile away. Pindar asked if we could see the town. We said we could see it.

"You can put up towns like that if you're a billionaire who's richer than me," he said. He thought that was pretty funny and laughed through his mask.

No one knew what he meant, and we got back in the truck and drove to the town. On the way we had to open and close gates, and then we were finally there. It was a little bit like being in a cowboy movie to be in the truck and drive down the main street of an old west town. There were livery stables, a boarding house, saloons, a bank, and a church. But no one there, no dogs or horses even, completely empty.

Dr. Glass: Was the person who owned that town around? Could you tell if he lived there? And this was out in the middle of nowhere?

They hauled that town from someplace else and rebuilt it there, completely rebuilt it. Pindar said he met the guy at a big party in New York, and that he was an asshole. We wanted to stop and look around a little more, look in some of the buildings, go upstairs, but Pindar said we didn't have time. After we left we stopped again and got out to look back at the town. While we were watching, a truck pulled up on Main Street and shined a spotlight in our direction. Pindar beeped the horn and the truck beeped back. When we got to the ranch it was late and the fire was almost burned out, the last of the coals.

It was the next day that Lawrence got sick and died. And two days later was when they took my blood.

Dr. Glass: You mean you decided to give them a sample?

After breakfast we were in the operating room and they had workmen who were installing something new. But it looked like they had too many. All of a sudden they were standing next to me, they were on me, holding me down. And that's when they took the blood. They took a pint and tested it and stored the rest.

"What are the odds?" Pindar said later on when they were done. He had his oxygen mask hanging from his ears and he was smiling. "What are the fucking odds?" he said again clapping his hands. Then he patted me on both shoulders like I was his son.

I knew what he was talking about. I knew why he was smiling, and I had wondered before, but the chances that he had the same kind as me were pretty small.

Dr. Glass: What was he referring to? What odds? Was he talking about your blood?

The golden blood, Pindar called it. Pindar had the same as me. Type O and Rh-null. He needed to have a new heart and couldn't do it until he found someone with his same type without the other stuff, without what they call the antigen.

Dr. Glass: Is that a rare type of blood, Francis? I don't think I've heard of that, but I don't know much about this area of the human body, hematology.

The Great Grandfather was given that kind of blood by Doctor a long time ago. Maybe it was a mistake, maybe that's all he could get. They didn't know as much about blood then. Only a few people in the world have it, like me and my sister, my half-brother. That was what Pindar was waiting for, what he was looking for. He thought maybe he could find it with the blood bank, but he never did.

After that he treated me different. He treated me, I don't know, like, like we were related.

Dr. Glass: But Francis, weren't you pretty upset that they

forcefully took your blood? And that they would have to do it again?

Oh, yeah, the faces. I looked around at the faces holding me down and I memorized them. I knew if I ever saw them again what that would mean, what would happen. And I looked at Pindar, at his face, his lips, his ears, his nose and neck and chin. In those few seconds I could see I would have to be watchful, and I would have to have a plan.

Dr. Glass: What was your plan, Francis? What were you going to do? And I hope it didn't involve violence or something like that. We still haven't closed the issue of the man in the club parking lot.

On the ranch, Pindar started giving me the easier jobs, taking me into town with him, talking with me about his business, the transplant business, OTP, and making sure Dr. Patel was training me to be a technician, which I thought was a good deal. I'd never done anything like that before. I didn't think I could, but Dr. Patel told me I could if I listened to him. At night I tried hard and studied in the bunkhouse, but I'm a slow reader, and I get distracted a lot. I studied the parts of the heart and the veins and arteries, the chambers, the valves. Dr. Patel gave me a plastic model and I kept it by my bed, touched it at night, held it like it was a doll or toy. And slowly, slowly, I began to learn.

When any of the cattle went down, when any of the calves got sick we sometimes opened them up and that was another way I got started. He showed me exactly where to cut on the skin, after the hide, light, then on the meat, clean, one stroke, how much of a stem to leave on the pulmonary vein, which artery to cut first, how to hold the heart or the liver or the kidneys so I didn't ruin them. Not that I would be doing the cutting or anything like that, but just so I knew. Then he showed me exactly how to stitch everything back on, to sew the organ, which is as important as cutting. I didn't mind the blood or any of that. Though I hadn't seen a lot of blood, I was always good with engines and I had good hands. I liked learning how to help Dr. Patel.

Dr. Glass: And did you understand there was an arrangement by Pindar for giving you special treatment? Did you know it then?

Not sure I knew it then, but I figured it out. When we would drive around he would tell me stories about growing up, about being a teenager and having to worry, having to sit out of everything, not having friends. He asked me how it was for me, that it must have been hard for me too, and I said I wasn't able to worry, I never had time to worry, even when there was trouble, even though I was different and always bigger and had the blood. Then he asked me if I would share the gold, stay at the ranch and donate blood, bank the blood, so if something happened to him, he had an operation, there would be a supply, and he wouldn't have to be afraid, wouldn't have to die.

Dr. Glass: This sounds a lot like hemophilia, which I know is different, but that's what it sounds like.

More people began to come to the ranch, all rich or famous, some I recognized. We got busier, sometimes five transplants a week, half of them hearts. And Pindar every day got a little sicker; I could tell when I was around him, next to him, listening to him breathing. So every three weeks I would give, every twenty-one days they would hook me up and I would give Pindar a pint of the gold blood. He would take me to town and buy me whatever I wanted to eat, steaks or anything with meat. He told me about how he got his money, and how he had to watch his partners in real estate, to make sure they didn't steal from him, take advantage. Pindar's not that big. He's a medium-to-small-sized guy, but he can be mean. He told me once he brought a gun to a meeting and shot up the copy machine and after that they didn't try to mess with him.

Dr. Glass: I thought it was only every two months you were supposed to give blood. That it might cause anemia otherwise.

At the ranch they had to make good food for the patients, they had to feed them, and so they made food with a lot of iron and protein in it just for them, and we got the same. But more spinach than steak.

Dr. Glass: How many people were there at any given time? Including patients, Pindar and Patel, the workers, who all was there?

Oh, I don't know now, maybe twenty-five. One night when all of us were standing around the fire singing, a woman walked up to the ranch. We stopped all of a sudden; we just froze like she was something from another planet. She came up from the county road, but told us she had tried to cross the railroad track and something caught her tire. She got a flat but drove on it anyway.

"Please," Pindar said, and he motioned for her to sit in his chair. She was tall, but not nearly as tall as me, maybe six feet, and she looked around at who was there and what we were doing. The cooks were out with us.

"Can you help me fix my tire?" she asked.

Pindar waited a moment and then said, "Why don't we hold off till morning, and you can stay in one of the guest rooms? I'll send Francis to help you."

He pointed at me.

"What happens here?" she asked. "What do you do here besides ranching?"

"We raise marijuana," Pindar said and laughed like a donkey, but with his oxygen mask on.

"Really?" she said.

"Why do you ask?" Pindar said.

"Just curious," she said and turned her back to the fire.

I wanted to walk down and fix the tire so she could leave

right away; she seemed nervous. I was afraid for her the more she stood around. And Pindar had a strange smile on his face.

"Show her to a room, Francis," Pindar said. "What is your name, miss?"

"My name is Evodee," she said looking around and drawing her coat up.

Pindar shook her hand with both of his and told her each of our names, like he was introducing a band.

"Is that French, Evodee?" Pindar asked. "Sounds French."

"Yes, I think it is. I never knew my parents though."

"An orphan, are you? Just like Francis. I think you're kind of an orphan aren't you, Francis?"

I didn't say anything about being kind of an orphan. But I could see her face when she turned to me, and the reflection of the fire in her eyes and cheeks. She looked like a young girl, but she was older.

She said something about it being late and dark and Pindar nodded.

"Francis," Pindar said, "show her to her room please. I think Miss Evodee's getting tired."

I showed her the guest rooms and the operating room, and explained about the transplants.

She nodded, said "Hmmm," and stood looking in the door but not wanting to go in.

"Where do you stay, Francis?" she asked.

I told her about the bunkhouse and that that's where Epiphanio, Javier, and me stayed, and that there were extra beds.

"Show me," she said.

At the bunkhouse, I showed her where Epiphanio and Javier slept, and where I slept. She touched their holy cards and pictures, looked at herself in the mirror, then stood by my bed. I could sense she felt comfortable with me, maybe because I was tall.

"Which one is open?" she asked.

This one, I said, pointing to Beatty's bed.

"I'll sleep there then," she said.

Pindar called me on the phone, but I didn't pick up. I knew he wanted to talk about the woman, Evodee. But I didn't want to talk to Pindar about her.

When Epiphanio and Javier came in, they looked at her, then looked at me, and went to bed with their clothes on. They weren't sure what to do.

After I'd washed my face and turned my reading light on, I tried to focus on the information Dr. Patel had given me, the workbook. But I had a hard time. The woman took her shoes off, hung her coat over the end of the bed, and climbed under the covers. Before long, she was snoring, making soft sounds through her teeth, like khhaa, khhaa, khhaa on the out breaths. I wanted to go and look at her, touch her face and hair, but I stayed on top of my bed until it got too cold. In a few minutes I dropped off and dreamed of Evodee. We were walking; we walked around over the ranch, and she talked, she was easy to talk to, but I didn't always know what to say. We went to the railroad tracks and she showed me where her tire had gotten the puncture and almost gotten stuck. I could see Pindar on a hill watching us with binoculars, following us. Again I wanted to touch Evodee, hold her hand, but she walked away, disappearing for a long time, and then the dream was over.

When I woke early in the morning she was gone. The door was open, the room was cold, and I thought Pindar had been there. It smelled like Pindar, and I wondered if he'd come and taken her. I threw my clothes on and ran out the door. Epiphanio and Javier were still asleep. I saw the kitchen people first and they just pointed to the road. They tried to tell me something in Spanish, but I didn't get it.

In a fast-walking way I hurried to where Evodee said she left her car. It was still dark, but I could see the sunlight coming in the distance. Would Pindar be there or had he taken her somewhere, done something to her?

My breathing made me almost sound like Pindar because I was nearly running. But I was afraid for Evodee, and when I got to the ranch gate I could see the car down the road, a small white car. The driver's side door was open and nobody was there. The tire on the passenger's side was torn up and flat. I looked for blood or hair, something, but there was nothing.

What to do, I said to myself, what to do? East and west on the road, I looked both ways. Maybe fix the tire, I said, at least that would be something, and she would need that. So I popped the trunk and got the tire out, jacked the car up. The sun came up on my back, and it felt good in the chilly morning.

When I finished I beeped the horn of the car a few times, but no one came and nothing happened. What if Pindar is doing something to her, operating on her right now? I shut the car doors and walked back to the house as fast as I could.

Pindar was still gone when I got there, and nobody was in the operating room or the dining hall. But Evodee wasn't anywhere to be found. The tall lady with the tire was gone.

Dr. Glass: Have you ever used a journal, Francis, ever written things down on paper?

Once, in a class in junior high, a teacher made us do it and at first I didn't like it, and then I kind of started liking it. Why?

Dr. Glass: Just wondering. Might consider doing it so you can try to remember the things in your life, some of these events that you're talking about, some of the things that have happened to you. Maybe some of your childhood memories, moving around, some of the painful things.

10.

Dr. Glass: I was just thinking, so many things happened after you arrived at that ranch. Beatty, Lawrence, the woman, giving up your blood. It has a very strange feel to it. I'm surprised you didn't leave right away. And I'm almost afraid to hear the rest. Have you been thinking about the boy? Has that been bothering you?

His mouth that said no, no, no. I see his face everywhere, in trees, in clouds, in shadows. I have nightmares about him all the time. He's reaching up to me, and I can't do anything. My headaches get worse when I dream of him.

Dr. Glass: I hope you can forgive yourself, Francis. Really, it wasn't your fault, as gruesome as it sounded. Something like this, I think, would be good to write down in a journal. I have some extras if you want one, just spiral notebooks, I give them to all my patients.

Not today, Dr. Glass, but maybe one of these days. I was just thinking about Pindar on the way over here. He liked to show old movies at the ranch. He showed them in the big dining room. After the woman left and he wouldn't tell me what happened to her, he showed a movie with the werewolf and Dracula, in Spanish. It was supposed to be funny, with these two guys . . .

Dr. Glass: Oh, you probably mean *Abbott and Costello Meet Frankenstein*? When I was a teenager I thought that movie was so funny.

. . . but I didn't think it was that funny. Pindar liked it and he laughed the whole way through, laughed and coughed, even though he'd seen it and didn't understand Spanish.

Epiphanio and Javier laughed too. They spoke Spanish to each other and pointed and drank beer and laughed, without coughing.

Dr. Glass: What did you say or do?

Pindar asked me if that was my father in the movie, if those people were part of my family. It was him joking, him trying to be funny again. I didn't pay attention and went outside and stood by the fire, then walked to the road. The woman's car was gone. I knew she wasn't there, but I said her name out loud, Evodee, Evodee, then went back to the house. When the fire died down I walked across the ranch in the dark, just the stars and moon. I thought it was awesome, totally cool.

Dr. Glass: Were you scared? I think I would have been scared, out there at night, all alone. Where were you going? And did it bring up a lot of issues? Being in the dark usually brings up issues for people.

I knew it would be late when I got there, but I wanted to walk to the old west town, walk through the buildings, maybe sleep there. The phone rang, it rang four or five different times while I walked. And I thought I might see the bear, but I only saw the cows.

Dr. Glass: Did the cows run away? Were they frightened?

Maybe the cows knew me, or maybe I didn't make much noise, or maybe they were asleep on their feet, but they didn't run away, only moved a little when they saw me. A funny thing, though; somewhere along the way the coyote came. The coyote followed me all the way to the town, walking next to me like a dog, and he waited on the edge of town.

Dr. Glass: You weren't afraid the coyote might bite you or attack when you weren't looking?

No, not really. On some of the buildings there were wires, I could see them going in and I had an idea; I knew what they were probably for.

Dr. Glass: What were they for, Francis? Security lights or electricity?

When Pindar took us before, I wondered how the truck with the beam knew we had been there. How it knew we were in the town. And then I looked in and saw the tiny cameras in some of the rooms. But in the livery barn there were no wires, and I climbed up to the second floor so I could see out, so I could see the coyote waiting like a dog.

On the floor I stretched out. I wanted to lay down and rest because I'd walked all the way. And when I did the coyote couldn't see me and barked like a singing dog, and came looking in the building for me. That night when I thought I would leave the ranch; leave and go somewhere, but I didn't know where. If I went to the city they might arrest me and there would be problems. Maybe I'd go back to jail. But I knew I had friends in Denver that might let me stay with them, help me out, because I had done things for them. This was before the basement.

Dr. Glass: Were you thinking of Hennie? Was she one of the friends who might help you? And were the problems you mentioned the man with the white shirt in the club parking lot? If we have the time you could say something about why you went to prison or jail in the first place.

Oh, no, I wasn't thinking of Hennie. These were other people who lived in the city but out of the way. People who worked mostly at night. Like Robeson and the people I'm with now.

Dr. Glass: And did you fall asleep in the town that night?

The coyote came into the livery and I called him. He wouldn't climb the stairs, he didn't know how, but he waited for me. He waited and lay down. I lay down too, walking along the roads. But soon the man from the old town came in his big truck, the caretaker. He saw us on one of the cameras, maybe a camera of the street, but he didn't know where we were. He called out from the loudspeaker on the truck, "Hey, you, better come out before you get in hot water."

The coyote heard him and barked, which was the wrong thing to do, because then he came to the livery. He had a gun with him, a pistol in his back pocket, and I could see him walking toward us. I wanted to tell the coyote to be quiet, but it was too late. I had to squat down so the man wouldn't see me. I thought he might shoot me.

He came inside the livery and the coyote went after him. I could hear it growling downstairs, and the man shot him, bang. It was a real loud noise inside that building. Shot him more than once too. He walked around the livery and called out again: "I had to shoot your dog, friend. I didn't have a choice, but nothing's going to happen. I don't want to have to do anything, but you can't stay here, just come out."

I stayed out of the way and he came up the stairs, I could hear him, one foot, then the other. And he kept talking: "Don't make me do something I don't want to do, come on out before something happens. You can't stay here; this is a private town. It's rich people and they don't want nobody here."

When I threw a piece of wood to make him look, he turned away and shot, and I knew I didn't have any choice. That's when I reached for him and stopped him from shooting me.

Then I tossed his gun away.

Dr. Glass: Francis, stop, I have to ask you: Did you kill him? I have to know this before we go on. You must tell me whether you killed him or not.

The coyote was dead when I went downstairs, and I touched his fur where there were holes, and there was lots of blood.

Dr. Glass: Please tell me, Francis. It's important that I know whether you killed that man, or we may have to terminate these sessions.

When he recovered, the man climbed down the stairs without saying anything, got in his truck, and drove away.

Dr. Glass: Francis, Francis, are you sure that's what happened? It sounded like it was more severe than that. You're not just saying that to stop me from asking questions and so I don't interrupt our sessions are you?

No, no, it's what really happened, Dr. Glass. So, when I started back it was late, I could see by the clock on the phone, and the sky was even clearer. It was very clear and a little cold. The sky was full of pictures, too, made from the stars, of animals or people, I don't remember what all. And there was a shooting star that crossed the sky and broke up, and I wanted it to be like a guide, or mean something special, but it turned out to be just a shooting star, which I liked anyway.

While I was walking I thought of the coyote and how he sang, and I started to sing like him. Owww-ow-ow. I sang and danced a little bit in circles, and then walked fast the rest of the way.

Dr. Glass: You still weren't scared or worried about something happening, an animal attacking you? I would have been.

Nah. I wanted to get back before it got light, and maybe the animals were more afraid of me, singing and making noise. I heard the night birds, the owls and the bats, some other little ones that flapped past, and my own feet, the sound of my feet shuffling and crunching, with the wind. I was hoping maybe the bear would come, walk with me, see me from a distance, be my friend, but I never heard him.

From the top of a rise I could see the ranch, with just a few lights, in the distance, and I knew then I only had a couple miles to go. It seemed like the road would be hard to see in the dark, and maybe it was a little bit, but mostly with the moon it wasn't.

In the bunkhouse I lay down for what seemed like only

a few minutes until I heard the Mexicans rustling around, cleaning up, and then I got out of bed and washed my face, under my arms, my teeth, and went to breakfast.

"Where did you go last night?" Pindar asked. "I don't think you were in the bunkhouse, were you?" He stood in front and faced me in the line.

Walking, I said. I was just walking.

"Long walk," he said adjusting the collar of my shirt. "Lots of animals to be afraid of. But not if you're in an old town, heh?"

The moon was out last night, I said, easy to see. Beautiful sky with a shooting star. Coyote sang to me. A perfect night.

"You didn't meet with somebody did you, talk to someone about the ranch?"

Let me think, I said. I don't remember seeing anyone, talking to anyone about the ranch.

"Almost time to give more blood, isn't it?" Pindar asked. "Getting to be that time."

Not for a few more days, I said. Tuesday, if I still have some left.

"Dr. Patel says you're doing fine, coming along learning about the heart and the other organs and how to be a technician."

I nodded but didn't say anything.

In the morning it began to snow, we didn't have any transplants, and just before I was going to drop off some hay for the cows, a sheriff's deputy drove up. He asked for Pindar and I pointed to the house.

When I was working out with the cows, Pindar called. He told me the deputy had asked whether any of the ranch people had been to the old west town the night before. If they'd seen anyone or encountered anyone while they were there. He told the deputy he would ask.

"I guess we should talk about what happened last night,"

Pindar said when he called. "If you saw anyone while you were out there."

He asked how long I'd be gone working that day, how long I'd be out, and I said I'd be back at dinner time or before, that I had a few more bales to drop off, that I had water tanks to deal with and was near the tracks and the bridge.

Just before we hung up, he told me the deputy asked if any of the ranch people carried weapons. Probably not, he said, but why? Because somebody shot a coyote and left it in one of the buildings out there. The deputy wanted to say something else, but he held off.

Dr. Glass: You're not carrying a weapon are you, Francis, a gun? That is strictly verboten in our counseling sessions or the office. Promise me you'll never bring a gun with you.

I promise, Dr. Glass. That day we had two surgeries. One in the afternoon and one in the evening, both kidney transplants. The first was a young guy, a young guy who went to college and whose parents were rich. The other, the second one, was a divorced woman, an older woman, whose ex-husband paid for her surgery. The guy went first and everything was ok; he did fine and there were no complications. But something happened to the woman.

Dr. Glass: Oh, no, don't tell me another something happened and you took her heart.

No, we left her heart. But when the operation started, when we began, her heart stalled, and it didn't act right. So Dr. Patel quickly had Javier get the defib machine from the cabinet. But when he tested it there was a problem with a resistor. It showed there was too much energy, too much electricity.

"We have a problem, a dysrhythmia on our hands," Dr. Patel said and turned to look at me. "See if you can fix this damn thing, Francis. We need to straighten this woman's heart out right away."

The voltage monitoring circuit continued, and it showed way too much electricity. I knew we could solve the problem temporarily, but I waited till Dr. Patel asked me if it was fixed, if it was working.

Dr. Glass: Did you know about those things, Francis? I think you said you knew about cars and machines but not things like that.

"Is that fucking thing back online yet?" he yelled after I'd fiddled with it.

No, I said, but I can make it work.

"Get up here," he yelled again. "This woman's heart is about to quit completely."

He asked me how I'd fixed the problem and I held my hands on her chest. Use the paddles, I said, use them through my hands.

"What are you talking about?" Dr. Patel demanded.

I'm not afraid, I said, electricity isn't a . . . it's not a problem for me.

The Mexicans were next to me, and I could see Pindar standing up in the gallery, waiting to see what would happen.

"Do it," Pindar shouted, "shock the son-of-a-bitch. We can't let her die."

After squirting gel on her chest, Dr. Patel called out "Ready," and put the paddles on my hands.

Ready, I said.

When he discharged the electricity it was a much higher voltage, and I jumped a little. I had to blink my eyes, but not too much. Her heart didn't straighten out, though; it wasn't back working right. So Dr. Patel put gel on my hands and did it again. It took a few seconds, then it started, the heart started back regular.

Everyone stood looking at me for a second to see if I would fall down, to see if I would collapse or have a problem with my own heart.

"What the hell was that?" Pindar yelled pointing at my hands. "What just happened?"

Dr. Patel ignored him and we went on with the operation, the kidney operation, and it went fine. No problems, and she never knew she almost died, and nobody told her. But I stood by waiting with the paddles while Dr. Patel and the Mexicans replaced one kidney with another, while they did the transplant. Dr. Patel laughed at the end. When it was all over he laughed and slapped me on the shoulder.

Dr. Glass: That is so, I don't know, interesting, Francis. What a story. And nothing happened to you at all? The electricity didn't harm you, burn you? Obviously somehow you must know about that or have done that before.

It's not the first time. There was a little buzz in my hands, and some in my body, in my ears, like I'd put my tongue on a battery, but I was all right and the woman was all right, and that night I slept pretty good, except for the dreams.

Dr. Glass: I can imagine. Your dreams were probably full of people being defibrillated.

There was someone who looked like me, someone who walked with his legs stiff and arms out, and lightning shooting from his hands and feet and head. He was bigger, almost twice as big, with scars and stitches, and in the shadows there were others like me, but they were having a good time, even singing by a fire, dancing.

Dr. Glass: What do you suppose gives you that strength, that ability to resist an electrical charge, Francis? It's like some kind of shield, and you never have to worry about going out in the rain or touching a socket.

The story that has been passed down, the story my family tells is Great Grandfather was the first. When the Doctor performed the original operation he used electricity, electricity, special blood, and transplants.

Dr. Glass: Electricity, transplants and special blood.

You've mentioned your Great Grandfather and the Doctor before and I'm not exactly clear who they are. Is this your actual great grandfather or someone from the foster homes, an older man you were involved with? And the Doctor you're referring to, is this your family doctor?

These are the original people, the Great Grandfather and the Doctor, the original Steins. So, changing the subject, while we were finishing with the kidneys, the kidney operations, I saw something moving on the floor in the corner, behind the canopy. But I never said anything or pointed. That would have made things worse. That would've made Pindar pretty . . .

Dr. Glass: Galvanism.

. . . he would've been upset. What is that, galvanism? Something in counseling?

Dr. Glass: It's the use of electricity to stimulate things like frog legs, maybe hearts or brains. Named after Luigi Galvani, an Italian scientist.

When everybody was gone, when the operating room was cleared out, I made sure no one was around, no one was there, and I looked by the wall. It was a mouse; I could see it was a gray mouse that'd snuck in somewhere and had gotten into the operating room. There are lots of mice in the country; the mice are everywhere.

With a paper cup and the broom, I managed to catch him, to scoop him into the cup and put my hand over the top. I could feel him on my hand trying to jump out. I got a look at him and he had big ears like Mickey's, big whiskers, and white streaks on his two front feet. In the bunkhouse I tied a string around his neck, like a little doggie, and put him in my shirt pocket. At night, when I was finished reading or playing with him, I put him in a shoe box with hay. The Mexicans liked him; they liked him and called him *El Raton*, like the city.

Dr. Glass: You caught the mouse and weren't afraid of him? I think mice are so nasty, with their little pooping.

When I went out to work on the ranch; when I got in the truck to drive out to the cows, I put El in my shirt pocket and pretty soon he stopped trying to get away. He liked to watch, to poke his head and front feet out and see what was going on.

Sometimes I kept him on my head, under my hat when I wore one, with the string tied to a button. Then I would take off my hat and there he was. People would point and be afraid, and I would act like I didn't know what they were talking about. What, I would say, ha-ha, what are you talking about? A mouse, on my head?

Pindar especially didn't like it. He didn't like it and called it vermin.

"That thing shits everywhere and carries disease. We can't have it around here, Francis."

He kept his distance; he stood back if he knew I had it. Finally, he told me it contributed in some small measure to the sanitation, the uncleanness of the whole environment, even though I never took him anywhere near the operating room or the dining room. I told him I gave Merk - that was the mouse's real name - a bath every week; gave him a bath and made sure his box was clean.

But one morning when I went to breakfast and left the mouse behind; one morning when I left him in his box and saved him a little food and brought it back. When I got back the box was gone and I immediately asked if Epiphanio or Javier had taken it; they had strange looks on their faces.

"Mr. Pindar told me," Epiphanio said. "He made me take it out and the *gato* right away found him."

My vision changed. I began to shake. I couldn't decide whether to do something to Epiphanio; to injure Epiphanio, or harm Pindar. I put my hands around Epiphanio's neck and he pleaded with me: "Pindar made me, Francisco. I promise. I liked *El Raton*; he was *muy guapo*."

Dr. Glass: I hope this isn't a story about more violence over a little mouse. I hope you're not going to say you killed Mr. Pindar or Epiphanio over a gray mouse.

I went to look for Pindar. He had an office, and I went to his office. But he wasn't there, he wasn't around. The cooks said he went into town to get something. Maybe groceries and other things. And I knew if I stayed there, we could possibly have a big fight. So I went out to do work; I went out on the ranch. One of the cows had caught its head in the barb wire and its hide was bloody around its neck. And then a stock tank needed water, there was a problem with the pump.

It became a nice warm day, maybe fifty degrees, with the wind down, a good day. At the bridge, I drove the truck over the tracks and got out and left it there. I was looking for Dr. Patel's snag for cars. Then I stood there and waited, and threw rocks at the bridge. Pindar tried to call me on the phone, every minute for a while. I thought maybe if the train slowed down for the truck I would get on. I would hop on the back somewhere, let the train hit the truck. And I could hear the sound, the noise that I'd heard before.

But it never came that day. I don't know why. And eventually, after I'd done more chores with the cows, after my anger had passed, I went back to the ranch.

11.

Dr. Glass: Did Pindar ever say anything about the mouse, or even explain why he did what he did?

Nothing, not a word and I was so pissed. Tuesday was blood day and we went to one of the high schools and parked the van outside. Pindar paid cash for the pints of blood, but it was Dr. Patel and the Mexicans who did all the work. I got people ready, the students and the people from the town of Doveless, and then passed them on.

The students liked to take pictures with me, selfies, touch my head to theirs, and when they asked my name, I said, Tallman, the name Pindar gave me.

Pindar liked to talk with people, ask them questions, especially the high school girls, and the women from town. But he always looked like he was sizing up their hearts, stroking his chin. When I watched him talking, his face and his mouth moving, his eyes blinking, his big crooked teeth, I wanted to punch him and push him out into the street.

Dr. Glass: It sounds like you were still very angry, maybe even with a touch of rage?

That was the Tuesday I was due to give blood, the golden blood, for Pindar. It was a nice day again and I sat outside so everyone could see; I was the guy who went first, even though I don't exactly like giving blood. And Pindar watched closely, noisy breathing while I sat next to the van and Epi took it from my arm. When I stared at Pindar, when I looked at him hard, he finally went away and did something else.

But while I sat there I wondered about how I could ruin the blood by putting something in it, or how I could open a hole and smear it all over Pindar. And I thought a lot about the plan, the plan for what I might eventually do to leave the ranch. I thought about walking home that day, too, but when I asked they said it was more than ten miles.

So I did everything to slow us down.

Dr. Glass: That's what we would call being passive-aggressive, Francis. Which isn't to say it wasn't justified, but that's what it's called.

Ok, passive-aggressive. Pindar got angry and told everyone to get in the van, goddamnit, that he had things to do.

"Francis," Pindar said, "get behind the wheel and drive this fucking vehicle."

He threw me the keys and I started the van, but then I got out and began looking under the seat, checking the tires, and all around. Being passing-aggressive.

"What the hell you looking for?" Pindar yelled. "The keys are in the goddamn ignition."

I thought I saw the mouse, I said, I'm pretty sure I saw him go under the seat, or under the vehicle, and we don't want him anywhere near that blood. Then I continued searching while the motor ran and Pindar swore and cursed and slammed the seat.

Dr. Glass: If I gave you a notebook, Francis, do you think you'd write some of these things down? Is that something you'd do between sessions? I mentioned it before, and even though you did it in school once, you might try it again to help you remember events and what people said, how you felt. I'd really like to encourage you.

All right, what the hell, one of these days I'll try it. Here's an example of something I might want to write about. The whole Evodee thing. While we were driving back to the ranch, before we left town, I thought I saw Evodee and I wanted to pull over and jump out, talk to her, see how she was doing, make sure nothing had happened to her. I circled the block and came back to where I saw her, but she wasn't there and her car was gone, too.

"What?" Pindar shouted. "What the hell did you drive around the block for?"

In the mirrors, I watched to see if I could see her coming out of someplace, if I could see her car, but I didn't see either her or the white car. If I got the chance, maybe one day or even at night, I would drive back to see if she was somewhere in the town.

When I looked back to watch Pindar in the back seat, I could see him touching the bag of blood, and grinning. One day, I realized, maybe sooner than later, he was really going to need that blood; he was going to need that blood and more, and because of that we were connected. But I didn't want to be connected to him. And I didn't know what to do. I didn't know whether to stay or go, and I felt like I had to continue at the ranch until I knew what was next or knew where I should be, and where I wouldn't get into trouble.

Even though it was winter, the weather became nice; it got warm, sixty degrees, and Pindar seemed to be happy. Dr. Patel was doing transplants almost every day, and I learned how to work in the operating room, knew when he needed something just by the look in his eyes. The Mexicans did most of the work, they knew more and were always right there, but I was getting it. And we had to hire more people to do the ranch work.

Pindar asked me to drive him one day when we had a break and I said I was busy, I had ranch work to do. He got in my truck anyway and we drove together without talking until he told me to stop. We were on the top of a rise and he got out and leaned against the hood of the truck.

"You know, Francis," he said, "the chances I'm going to find someone with an O-negative Rh-null heart are about zero."

I nodded at him, then didn't say anything. It was true, but I didn't care.

"You wouldn't be willing to give yours up would you?" he asked laughing. When I looked at him he said, "Joke, just old Pindar making a joke."

Ha-ha Pindar. Pindar the funny guy. Pindar the clown. The thing of it is, when he laughed, he showed his teeth, like a skeleton, especially his pointed teeth on the side.

"Partly the reason I wanted us to go for a ride," he said, "was to talk about an approach should I ever go down or when it's time for a transplant and I'm out of it."

He actually looked like he was ready to go down. He looked like he could have collapsed at any moment, and his breathing was noisier, like he had a bad cold.

Dr. Glass: Did you think he was dying? Were you afraid he might die right there?

I was and I wanted him to get in the truck so we could go back. I didn't want to have to take care of him, resuscitate him, put my mouth on his mouth, or pump his chest. I didn't like him or trust him. Maybe he wasn't going to die that night or the next day, but he was going to die sooner than later because there were no hearts around for him, and mine was going to stay where it was.

He patted me on the shoulder, stood close and said, "The whole having to forcefully take your blood from you, and even the mouse thing, I know that was pretty harsh and I apologize, but I have my reasons, believe me I have my reasons. I should have said something in advance, but, hey, I didn't."

Then he put his arm around me and began to cry. "Look, the truth is I think of you like a son, like I'm your father, and I want you to work the ranch and help out in the operating room, eventually take over the ranch, make it your own. I don't have any children, no sons or daughters, but you could be the child I never had."

I looked at short little Pindar, reaching his arm up to me, barely able to touch my shoulder, trying to make his pitch and I wanted to believe him; I wanted to trust him. I could've used something like that then.

"When the time comes to get the new heart, I want you right next to me, holding my hand, protecting me, making sure I get the right supply of golden blood. Can you promise that you'll stick around till then? At least promise me that."

He was pleading and he had his arm around my waist, squeezing me. It was, I don't know, it was so crazy it made me want to laugh.

On the way back to the ranch house I thought I saw the bear. I thought I saw him off on the side and I flipped the lights to bright.

"What's up?" Pindar said when I slowed down. He'd been looking kind of shaky next to the door.

It's the bear, I said. You didn't see him?

"If there is a bear, which I doubt, why would we want to slow down for him?"

He's like a good luck charm, I said. He's been here ever since I jumped off the train.

"I didn't see him last time you said something, and I didn't see him this time. You're dreaming, Francis, you're dreaming. Next thing you know you'll be asking if he can sleep in the bunkhouse."

We drove back with the windows down, and I looked for the bear. I looked for him all around and thought I heard him, trotting along with his big paws, even thought I smelled him once, but never saw him. Pindar fell asleep in his corner and I drove slower, looking at the sky, looking at the patches of trees, waiting for the bear. When we got back I let Pindar stay asleep in the truck and went inside. I didn't exactly expect him to, but the bear never showed.

When I saw Dr. Patel I asked how Pindar was doing, how long he had?

"It is a race," Dr. Patel said. "The chances are not good. Because of you we at least have enough blood if we must do the operation, but no donor for a heart yet."

Earlier, while we were standing next to the truck out on the ranch, he put a thousand dollars in my shirt pocket, just one bill, and when I looked at it later I realized it was the most money I'd ever seen. But at first I thought it was fake, maybe like Halloween money, and like he was making another joke.

Dr. Glass: Not that this is important to our session, but here's a bit of trivia: Do you remember who's on the thousand-dollar bill?

No, I don't. One of the presidents. Pindar folded the money and put it in my pocket, and I waited till I was inside the bunkhouse to look at it, to take it out. It wasn't Jefferson, but I remember looking at it close up, and saying his name, but I can't remember it now.

Dr. Glass: No, you're right, it isn't Jefferson. Give up? It's Cleveland, Grover Cleveland.

What to do with a thousand dollars? Buy a car or a pickup, go back to Denver and get a room, give some to Evodee? That's what I was thinking.

That day a fat man had come from Germany to get a liver transplant. He was big, maybe four-hundred pounds, and we thought the table would collapse.

He was a laugher; he laughed while he waited and we got him ready, and he sounded like someone trying to laugh with a motor running.

"Here is a fellow," he said with his motor-laugh, in a German accent, and pointing at me, "here is a fellow who is much bigger than me, and less attractive too."

He was maybe six feet, and he had blotchy white-pink skin, with a hairy, hairy chest, and everyone laughed with him; they thought that was funny. We had to shave him. But I told the Mexicans I didn't want to do it; I didn't want to have anything to do with the fat, pink German.

That man had waited a long time, and finally Pindar found a liver for him in South America. We never knew where the organs came from exactly, and Pindar kept it that way. We hardly ever knew which country and which town or whether it was a man or woman, or even a high-school boy.

The German owned a manufacturing company that made things no one else made, and that's why he was rich, he said. And I said to myself, That's why you're so rich, and so fat.

But here's the thing: he died. He died right after Dr. Patel cut him open. Dr. Patel said his heart was too small and couldn't take the stress of the operation, and his weight made it worse. Plus they found cancer on his pancreas. When he died he just kind of shuddered; he shuddered, turned to one side, and then it looked like he gave up and died. But I didn't much care about the German.

Dr. Patel tried everything, even defibrillation, massaging his heart but nothing worked. And he was pretty upset, threw things around. With the dead German there on the table. Cursing and throwing things.

Dr. Glass: God, it must have been, you know, kind of weird having that German man lying on the table, and still cut open.

We couldn't stop that day, even though Dr. Patel needed a break, because there were people waiting and organs waiting, so we had to get ready and do one early the next morning anyway. And when Dr. Patel started operating, his hands were shaking; his whole body was shaking, and I had to step up to his side, step up and hold him. The Mexicans kind of took over and had to tell him what to do; do some of it themselves.

After the transplant in the morning, I had ranch work I needed to get to, and I thought I would disable Dr. Patel's trap at the railroad crossing when I had a chance. From the barn I got a chainsaw and axe, plus a big pry bar. Along the way, one of the small herds needed feed, silage, and when I was there I saw that a calf had gotten baling wire wrapped around its hoof and he was limping and mooing in distress. The wire had cut into him and I had to take clippers to get it off. He needed to have it salved, too, to keep it from getting infected. The mother acted like she wanted to butt me, she made noise and I thought she might ram me, until she figured out I was helping.

Dr. Patel's trap was still working and I got the electric eye on the crossing-light pole to turn on. With the chainsaw I cut the top part of the trap off and with the pry bar I disabled the rest of it. With the snippers I removed the electric eye and just when I finished, the train came. It was the same one that I'd ridden on. In one of the empty box cars there was a small group of men sitting in the door, hanging their feet out. I waved and they waved and the engine blew its horn.

As it started to get dark, I decided I would drive into Doveless and try to find Evodee, see if she was there. But I didn't want to cross through the ranch, the short-cut; I would have to drive all the way around, which would take about twenty minutes longer.

The road followed the creek part way, and I could see the red willow starting to come back, starting to sprout. A big power line crossed the road, and the towers looked like a metal giant marching across the hills, holding rope over its shoulders. It was late in the afternoon, almost evening, when I drove into Doveless and rode around. Cars were parked at an angle and there was a small town square with stores around it. In front of the café was the white car; it was Evodee's car.

From inside the truck I could see tall Evodee working. She was a waitress; she was serving people, carrying plates. I thought I would go in and order something to eat. From the street Evodee looked younger, like she was thinner, or maybe it was just her hair was pulled back. I couldn't bring myself to just walk right in, to go in alone and sit down, so I walked around the square, looked in store windows, but watched the café from wherever I was.

When I was on the opposite side, the same deputy who

came to the ranch drove past and then stopped. He parked and called out to me.

"Hey," he said without getting out. He motioned and waited for me to come to the car. "Don't you work on that ranch I stopped at a few days ago?"

Yeah, I said, I work on the Pindar ranch.

"Know anything about the man who was killed at the old west town? Somebody killed a man out there and left him."

Was there a man who was killed there? I asked. Pindar only told us about the coyote.

"You got any I.D. on you?"

No, sorry, I forgot it at the ranch.

"What's your name?" he asked.

Francis, I said.

"No last name, just Francis, like one of those big rock stars?"

Stein, I said, my last name's Stein.

"Let me run a check on you, Stein, to see if you got any problems with the law."

For a minute I thought I should run away or jump in the truck and drive, but I waited. The deputy talked back and forth to the base and spelled out my name.

"Kind of a tall guy, aren't you?" he said while we waited. "How tall do you suppose you are?"

Six-eight, six-nine, I said.

"A foot taller than me," he said. "Where you from?"

Denver, I said, mostly Denver.

The base called back and the deputy said, "Ok, ok."

"Just thought you'd come into Doveless and get a taste of city life?"

No, sir, just thought I'd stop at the café, go in and get something to eat.

"Try the enchilada pie," the deputy said. "I had some at lunch, the special. And the new girl Evie is kinda special too."

I wanted to tell him it was Evodee, the woman's name was Evodee, but I held back.

"You're free to go on your way," the deputy said. "Take care."

He drove away slowly and I finished walking around the square. It was a little surprising. Some of the stores had their windows boarded up or for rent signs posted. When I got back to the truck I found some paper and a pencil in the glove box. I didn't want to go into the café; I couldn't go into the café, so I thought I would write Evodee a note.

In the truck I turned on the radio and listened to news about agriculture. Then I tried to say something: Dear Evodee, I wrote, but I didn't know if I should say dear or even if she would remember me. I sat there till the street lights came on and the café turned its sign on. Maybe I would ask if her car was ok, or maybe I would see if Pindar had bothered her, or maybe I would say I was worried when she left the bunkhouse early, or maybe I would ask if she wanted to come out to the ranch again, have sandwiches somewhere.

In the end I wasn't able to write one word; I couldn't write anything. So I folded the paper up and wrote her name on the outside. On the inside I just printed my name, Francis, with a phone number, and put the note under the windshield wiper. I took it away once and put it back. Then I drove around the square, watching Evodee, and finally, after circling three times, I drove back to the ranch.

In the truck I drove the paved roads back, then onto our dirt road, but I didn't want to. I wanted to just keep going, never stop, drive around the world.

12.

That night, when I was already in the bunkhouse, when I was almost asleep, I decided to put on my clothes and go outside. No one was awake on the ranch, and I'd made a few notes earlier in your notebook, the one you gave me.

Dr. Glass: Oh, that's good. Were you feeling unsettled? Were you ill at ease with yourself? Were you fearful of something?

Well, I guess I was unsettled. When I got outside there were still coals left in the fire and a little bit of heat, but not much. And while I was standing on the outside edge, while I was thinking, I looked up at the grain silo, with its red light on top, and I decided to climb it, to get up there.

Dr. Glass: How tall was this silo, how many feet?

Not sure. But the big silo had a ladder that went all the way along the side, maybe fifty feet, and my hands were really cold from the metal by the time I'd climbed all the way up. The silo reminded me of a fat rocket, one that wasn't ever going to take off.

Dr. Glass: You weren't afraid of slipping or being up there in the dark?

I was a little afraid. And right when I got on top it started to snow lightly and the clouds covered the moon. It shined through anyway but fuzzy. I stood next to the red light at the top and it made my face and hands, my whole body, turn red. It was unreal with the snow and the light, being up that high, looking at the dark country all around.

While I was there I had to pee. I had to go real bad, so I just pulled it out and took a leak. But I lost my balance while I was peeing and slipped down to the edge, fell down and almost slid off. Sounds kind of funny when I'm talking about it now. But at the last second, I stopped, or something stopped me.

Dr. Glass: What do you mean, something stopped you? Say more, Francis, about what happened? What kind of something?

It was like someone was stopping me, like they had a hold of my coat, and I thought for sure I was going off the edge, that I was going to fall to the ground and no one would find me.

Dr. Glass: But you didn't, and you're here today. Did you stay on top of the silo or climb down right away? That's what I would have done.

Because it was wet, I had a hard time clawing my way back up to the light, in the center of the dome, which blinked two or three times before I got there. I thought maybe someone had turned it off and on, off and on, but I looked around and no one was there. It's Pindar, I said to myself, but then I said, No, Pindar would have turned it off and left it off so that I was completely in the dark.

I held onto the light, it was warm, and sat there for thirty minutes. I wasn't cold but I started to get a little damp. If I stretched my arms all the way out, I thought, spread my wings, I could fly off this silo, fly all over the ranch like a night hawk, and land in one of the fields. With one leg on either side of the light for stability, I stood up. My legs were shaky, they were jittery, but I was able to stand straight, hold my arms up like a boxer, before I got down on my knees and crawled to the ladder.

From the silo, I could see the pond that Pindar used for fishing with a small boat on it. In the evening or warmer afternoons, I had seen him out in the middle, sitting in the small boat, sometimes catching fish, sometimes just sitting there holding his pole. And I thought I would go to the pond and get in the boat, too, paddle out to the middle and sit there. The snow had stopped and the clouds had cleared off a little, so it was pretty bright.

The boat was hooked to a chain and the chain was attached to a cement anchor. It was muddy around the pond, and I got in the boat and shoved off. We had seen deer and antelope drinking the water at the shore, and I paddled around to see if any of them were there. This little lake was about the size of a football field. It was the same length and width, with a beachy place and a picnic table and barbeque, and lots of bushes.

While I paddled I could see the silvery bubbles from the boat spreading into the water and it looked like fish at first, swimming away. Then I began to see actual fish, rising up, wondering who this guy was so late at night floating around. The tiny shoosh of the boat, I liked hearing that sound in the water as I glided along, and I tried to be very quiet, stroking the paddle softly against the water, trying hard not to let it knock the boat.

Out in the middle I sat on the bottom of the boat and slumped between the seats. Nothing is wrong tonight, it's a good night, I thought, no trouble is happening, forgetting that I'd almost fallen off the silo. Maybe this would be the time to walk away, leave the ranch, forget about any kind of plan to get back at Pindar. I had some money in my pocket, plus Pindar's thousand-dollar bill, now would be the right time to go to Denver, get a room somewhere, get another job, but not with Hennie and the club.

Dr. Glass: Aside from almost falling off the silo, it sounds like you really were having a good night. I'm interested to hear more about the pond. What else happened? And when you talk about the pond, incidentally, your face gets relaxed and you smile.

As I sat in the boat watching the sky, I must have fallen asleep, because when I opened my eyes again it was morning and the sun was trying to come up. I paddled to the shore, rechained the boat, and stepped into the mud. Later on, if it wasn't too busy and I'd finished my chores and there were no transplants, I would drive somewhere and sleep, have a nap in the truck.

Walking back to the bunkhouse, I saw the jet fly over and land at the airport. After I'd showered and changed, I went to the dining hall to get something to eat. Dr. Patel was there eating alone and he called me over to his table.

"Pindar found a heart for himself in Canada and it just arrived. We need another pint of blood to be on the safe side."

I just gave blood a few days ago, I said. It's probably too soon.

"Drink lots of fluids and eat protein for the next few days. It should be all right. And Pindar wants you there next to him for the operation."

Doing chores and taking a nap weren't going to happen. When I saw Epiphanio at breakfast he had a strange look on his face.

What? I said. Is there a problem, something to do with Pindar's heart?

"*No hay problema*," Epiphanio said shaking his head. Then he tapped me on the heart and waved me off with his hand. We left the dining hall together.

When we separated, when we walked away from each other, I looked back at him and he was staring at me. I stood there thinking he would say something, that he would add something, but he didn't and I went on. I tried to figure out what the look on Epi's face meant, but I couldn't.

The car came up from the jet and brought Pindar's new heart. The heart was in a special cooler in the front seat. Someone I thought I recognized, but wasn't sure from where, was the driver and the deliverer. There were three others in the back seat of the car.

And then I knew.

I'd seen the men before.

It came to me.

I recognized their faces.

And I could see Epi's face again, that look.

Why didn't I think of it? Son of a bitch.

Dr. Glass: What did you know, Francis? Why didn't you think of what? Was it Evodee's heart? No, it couldn't have been.

Neither of the two Mexicans were in the bunkhouse when I got there. Nobody was there. I packed my bag as quick as I could and had to leave some things. Pindar, I whispered clinching my teeth, Pindar.

From the barn I got a can of gas, a full can that was for the chainsaws. Outside I saw the four men coming from the operating room looking for me. They went to the bunkhouse.

Dr. Glass: I hope you're not getting ready to tell me what I think you're going to tell me.

I started on the far side and lit the fire right away. I lit the fire around the operating room.

Dr. Glass: Oh, Francis, that's not what I thought you were going to tell me. Oh, god, tell me you didn't burn all those people up.

I poured it on the doors and at the bottom to make it hard for them to get out. Then the four men came and tried to stop the fire, but they only had water from a small hose. Pindar, I whispered again, Pindar.

I threw the can on the roof and it exploded; it exploded and there was another fire. People were running everywhere and I started a truck. In the mirror I could see the building burning up, and I hoped that Pindar was inside, on the table. But I didn't know.

On one of the dirt roads I drove real fast to the old west town and parked outside so the cameras wouldn't see. The back door of the livery was open and I went in. My phone rang and I ignored it. I searched for the dead coyote, but he was long gone and there was only a spot of his blood on the floor.

My phone rang again and it was Dr. Patel.

"What did you do?" he shouted in a high voice. "Where are you now? Are you still here? The sheriff is looking for you. You have done great damage."

Where is Pindar? I asked. Is Pindar alive?

"Did you think he was going to take your heart? Who told you that? Did someone tell you that? He only needed your blood as a back-up."

Who were the men? I asked Dr. Patel. What did they want?

"They were only there for safety, for Pindar's safety, and now. . . ."

Is Pindar alive? I asked. Did Pindar survive?

Dr. Patel hung up the phone.

They would be coming for me, I thought. They would eventually know where I was and come for me. With the matches I had left over, I threw big wads of lit paper in every building and some of them I had to light twice. Because it was all wood, the old west town went up quickly, and I had to get away because of the heat. Standing on the top of the truck, the flames made a beautiful fire and it roared like an animal, like a lion not like a coyote. That day the buildings collapsed one after the other in a kind of fire-splash. And then I was away from all of that place, that country.

Part 3

Chapter 13

The green ranger's truck stopped and I got ready to run. He rolled the window down and called out to me.

"Hey, you look like you could use a ride. Need a ride somewhere? I'm going back down the hill into town."

I thought it might be a trick and waited.

Yeah, I said, I could use a ride.

"You see that bear?" the ranger said when I walked up to the truck. I shook my head.

"I'm surprised you didn't see that bear. It's one of the ones that've been getting into the trash and we're probably going to have to euthanize him. But in the meantime, he gave us a good chase out into the forest where the trucks can't go. We been tracking that boy for a while. The deputies surprised him back up there by the lake somewhere."

Maybe that's not the one you're looking for.

"He had a tag on his ear. I could see that. He's the one all right."

The truck heater felt good. My teeth were chattering. I was shivering.

"How'd you come to be out here?" he asked.

I was hiking around the lake and fell down the hill, I

said. Probably hit my head on something. Lucky I didn't sprain my ankle.

"You look like you got tangled up with a pile of leaves," he said. "And you smell like you been sleeping with that bear."

Oh, I said hanging back a second, well, I was working on my car and probably got oil or brake fluid on my clothes.

"Let me get that horse blanket out of the back," he said. "You're looking pretty chilly."

The ranger stopped the truck and got the blanket and gave me a stocking cap too. But it took me a while to begin to get warm.

"Did you see all those deputies," the ranger asked. "Flashing lights and everything. Flew right past me at first."

I saw them circling the lake, I said, and that's about when I fell down.

"Maybe you got distracted and that's what caused you to fall."

Possible, I said. Any idea what they were after?

"Never can tell about these deputies. I try to ignore them. Probably somebody didn't pay their parking ticket."

We drove without talking for a minute, with only the base radio making noise, and then he asked if I was working, if I had a job.

I'm looking, I said. I've been working on a ranch out near Doveless.

"That ranching can be some hard work. Ever done any fire work?"

No, I said, and was ready to add that I'd started a few, but held back.

"You might be too big to be a smoke jumper," he said, "but it's possible we could cut you some slack, too. For sure you'd be able to get on a handcrew, start out that way."

How do I find out about that? Who do I ask about that kind of work?

"You could start by asking me. I'm looking for a couple more jumpers."

I said I was interested and could use the money. He asked me my name and shook my hand.

"You got your I.D. with you? We could probably start the paperwork today, if you want."

I told him I forgot my identification in Denver and he said that I'd need an I.D. eventually, but that they could do something temp. Lots of Native kids never had an I.D. and all I'd need to do is swear on an affidavit.

"This kind of work can change a guy, if you let it. You interested in that sort of thing?"

I might be, I said, thinking about it. I just might be.

At the office, Roger told the secretary to help me get started making an employment file and that I would fill out an affidavit and bring my I.D. later.

"This is for my crew," he said. "And he's got lots of good ranch experience as background."

I'd become drowsy and had to sit down. The cold made my wounds not hurt so much, but as I got warmer they started to throb like a bad headache.

Roger said, "Kinda quick but if you're ready we could do a physical? I think the doctor is still in."

I said I was ready, but in a way I was surprised to even be alive and wondered what the doctor would say about the gunshot wounds.

"Is Dr. Joan still in her office?" Roger asked the people who were there.

Yes, someone said, she's here till 4:30.

I didn't want to see a woman doctor, but thought I'd wait to say anything.

Dr. Joan came out and was wearing purple-green colors that clashed with her off-color shoes and rhinestone glasses. They handed her my file and she looked at my name, looked at me, and told me to follow her into the office. Dr. Joan was an old woman and she walked like her feet hurt, plus she was good-sized, more hefty than tall.

"Francis," she said once we were in her office, "a large person like yourself has probably taken a fair amount of ribbing about that name before, hmmm?"

I started to say it was a big problem in high school, but she asked me to strip to my shorts before I could.

"I'll just work on your file over here and if you're at all modest, please feel free to use one of the robes there on the back of the door."

When I reached for the robe she turned around and noticed the wounds in my arms and leg. "Ahhh," she said, and then "we better take a look at those."

Examining them with her thumbs, she said, "I'm quite sure these were accidental, yes, maybe hunting? Not something from a shoot-out at a bar or trouble with the law. You're in luck, though. They're only superficial. We can take care of these right here in the office. Fortunately, it's been cold, otherwise you might have bled to death or gotten an infection. We're going to need to numb these sites and clean them up before we surgically remove the projectiles. I can see two of them, and the third is hiding a little deeper. All of them will need stitches, though. You'll have to have at least a few day's rest before doing any strenuous activity, like training to be a smoke-jumping firefighter. And you'll have to keep them wrapped with ointment on them."

She asked me if I was ok with all this, and I said I was. She said we'd finish the physical as soon as she took care of the injuries. The physical mostly consisted of questions about TB or scarlet fever, AIDS, then looking into my eyes with a light, my ears, and then she said she had to check for hernia. She got one of the men to come in when she did, but I was still pretty embarrassed. When he left she said everything was strictly confidential, did I understand that? I said I did and thanked her. Dr. Joan came off as a little crusty, but I liked her.

"You need a place to stay?" Roger asked when we were done and he'd told me when to report and where.

I lied and said I thought I had a place, and he told me they had an empty cabin with four bunks, but the heat wasn't on yet, though there was a wood stove. If I wanted to use it, the key was above the door, and there were extra blankets in the closet.

I hadn't had anything to eat since the Christian breakfast, and I walked out of the office with Forestry clothes and looking for someplace I could get something to munch on, not be too obvious. McDonald's was down the road a hundred yards and there was a sandwich place next door with booths. I checked my pockets for money and found a still-wet ten. Whichever restaurant the deputies were least likely to visit, I thought, was the best one.

In the sandwich place there were two Nicaraguans behind the counter with hair nets who could speak ok English, but not great.

"Especial tonight," one of them said, "three for one, with ships, drink and cookie. Store close tomorrow."

Store's completely closed after tonight? I asked.

"Finish."

I ordered the tuna salad, a roast beef, and a roast turkey, all foot long. I knew I would need something to eat later. I'd finished one and a half and started to wrap the unfinished ones up when a deputy came in.

"Look at this," the deputy said pointing at me. "This guy has the right idea. He ordered foot longs. What did you get?"

With my hand covering the side of my face and pulling

my hat down, I turned away from him and said tuna, roast beef, and turkey.

"That's what I'm going to do," he said, "exact same thing."

While he ordered I walked out, but before I could get very far, he called to me.

"Hey," he said, "you drop something?"

He was holding a five-dollar bill.

Oh, thank you, I said, trying hard not to show my face and scrunching down. It was another wet one and he shook it out and handed it to me. But the best thing is he didn't recognize me.

The Forestry cabin was two or three miles up a paved road that led south from the small strip mall, and maybe a quarter-mile or so off on a two-lane track. When I got there I was very tired and still pretty nervous. Inside it was chilly but there was blocked-up wood neatly stacked outside and some next to the stove. Maybe Roger forgot he'd loaned the cabin out.

On one of the beds there was an extra blanket, as though someone either was sleeping there or forgot to put it back. The bunk I picked was by the window, but away from the stove. Getting my shoes untied was a major task, and I fell back on the pillow when I got them off and went sound asleep.

The small fire in the stove was what woke me, the cracking and popping. And the fact that there was someone sitting at the kitchen table eating my sandwiches. The room was warm.

When I'd cleared my eyes I said, What the hell are you doing?

"Which part?" he asked. "The stove or the sandwiches."

It was an old man with a white beard, like you might see in a fairy tale. And he had a hard hat next to him on the table.

The sandwiches, I said. What are you doing eating that

sandwich? I was saving those for dinner. I still had a hell of a headache, and my arms and leg hurt where Dr. Joan removed the bullets. A handful of aspirin would have been good.

"Not to worry about the food. I got plenty. Roast trout, salad fixings, vegetables, dessert."

You got all that here?

"No," he said laughing a gurgly kind of ho-ho laugh, "but it sounds good. Mostly macaroni and cheese. Cans of pinto beans, Velveeta, Gatorade. You used to eating fancy?"

I'm used to eating my own stuff, or noodles and burgers when I'm in the city. Pancakes with the Christians.

"You look familiar," the old man said. "Where do I know you from?"

From the TV, I said. You been watching the goddamn TV lately?

I thought I'd just blurt the whole thing out if he asked any more questions. And then throw his stuff outside and chase him off if he kept up.

"Nah, don't watch much TV, 'cept if I'm in a bar and they got the NFL on, or the news. Ever work on these logging crews or done any hardhat construction?"

I was living in Denver and got into some trouble with the cops just before this. They're still looking for me pretty hard. Before that I was out on a ranch near Doveless.

"Doveless, now there's a name. A city without doves. We used to drive through it when I was a kid and my folks lived out there. What'd you do, shoot one of 'em?"

You mean the cops? Well, as a matter of fact I did. But I didn't have any choice. He shot Poletta twice and would've shot me. I choked him down and then shot him with his own gun. On the TV they're saying I shot both of them, but I only shot him. And I didn't really want to. I wanted to spend a nice night with Poletta on the blanket. But he shot her when she came down the stairs with a caulking gun. She

135

was taking a shower. I'd been having one of my migraines for a week.

"The cops shot your girlfriend?"

Twice, I said. Killed her right there. Another one that didn't matter.

"That's intense. And then what?"

Then I torched the place. A new house and I torched it. With both of them still in it. I didn't want them to find her there, see her.

"Man, remind me not to piss you off. You ok with the fire in the stove aren't you?"

The old man was smiling like he was trying to kid me.

I'm ok with the fire, I like a good fire, just as long as you don't eat any more of my sandwiches.

"You have more sandwiches? What kind?"

I asked what his name was and he said Roy Sturm. "They call me old Roy." And he asked my name.

Francis, I said, Stein.

"Probably don't go by Frank, do you? Too obvious."

The old man had a funny way of tilting his head when he talked, like someone from India, especially when he asked questions.

Most people don't remember this, I said, but it was just the Doctor who was named Frankenstein. They mostly referred to his creature as monster and wretch. How would you like to be called a wretch, whatever that is. Long ago the Grandfathers took the name, adopted his name. My father broke it apart and dropped the Frank, except when he named me Francis.

"I just remember all that electricity coming out of him. But I liked Wolfman the best, so much hair."

Galvanism, I said.

"What's that, galvanism? Sounds like something related to women."

The psychologist told me it was about using electricity to stimulate things, like frogs or creatures.

"So there were other Franks before you? Were they all tall like you?"

A whole line of us, some even taller. But it might stop here. Because there's just me, a half brother on the West Coast somewhere, and my sister, and she doesn't like men.

"All of you get into trouble?"

Seems like. One way or the other.

"You been to see a psychologist?"

Yeah, I said, in Denver, trouble sleeping and headaches.

"Where did you grow up?"

Everywhere. They would take us away and then my parents would get us back. Then we'd move to the next state and get into trouble somehow. We lived in Denver a lot, though. Do the Forestry people know you're staying here?

"Not that I can tell. In a month there'll be some young cubs in here and I'll have to find another place, or sleep out. You sleep out much?"

Only if I have to. Roger from Forestry said it was ok for me to stay here. I might go to work for them.

"I did see your picture. I said I didn't but I did. I wanted to check out what you'd say and what kind of person you were. The way they talk about you on TV makes it sound like you're a crazed cop killer."

I didn't want to kill that cop but he shot Poletta, and I was in love with Poletta.

"What kind of name is Poletta?"

A good name. Don't say anything about it because I'm still thinking of her.

"Sounds like a name black people might have. Like a cross between Paulette and polenta."

I thought I said not to say anything. You want to sleep out in the cold?

"Sorry, Francis," old Roy said, and he looked like he meant it. "There's an outhouse in the back just in case you have to use it, and I got a bucket of water and soap out there for washing hands and such."

Where'd all this wood come from? I asked.

"I cut it up myself," he said. "It's my thing. I'm a wood-cutting son of a bitch. I try not to burn too much, though, try not to attract attention."

What do you do for money? I asked.

"Odd jobs," he said. "Splitting wood, putting up fences, re-digging wells, mostly forest contracts."

And you don't have a permanent place? How about some kind of senior living? You're a senior citizen aren't you?

"You're thinking I'm old just 'cause I got this white beard, right? How old do you think I am?"

Oh, I don't know, maybe 65 or 70.

"Man, I'm just a young guy of 60."

Must be all that hard living.

"I'm 85," he said. "All my people live to be 90 and a hundred."

Mine too, I said, as long as they don't get killed first.

"Regarding that senior living, I'd go crazy in one of those places. All that ass wiping and shitty food, drooling and pissing your pants. Even when I nearly freeze to death, which happens regularly, I still prefer being out, or sneaking in, like to this place, when I can."

Seems like we have two secrets to keep.

"What are they?"

You hiding out here in the cabin and me on the run from the Denver cops.

Old Roy poured us glasses of Gatorade and we clinked them together.

You ever see a bear out here? I asked.

"Black or brown?" he asked.

Brownish black, I said. Dark brown. The ranger said he has a tag in his ear, but I never saw a tag.

"This bear belong to you? He your pet bear or something?"

He's been with me from the time I was on the train, up to the ranch, to when I fell down the hill and rolled under the shed. Not exactly a pet bear. More of a friend.

"That why you smell like you do?"

Nah, that's from repairing something on the car.

"I've heard one in the woods when I've been working, and seems like he's gotten into a cabin or two when I wasn't there, looking for food, but I've never had a confrontation with him. What makes you think it's the same bear?"

Don't know. Just seems like it. Probably not, in reality, 'cause how could he get here?

"How'd you get from Denver out here? Weren't they looking for you?"

Got a ride with a drunk lady who was coming this way. Probably a bad idea, 'cause they stopped us in Silverthorne when they checked her plates.

"Was she drunk behind the wheel?"

I was driving and they surrounded the car. I kicked her out and tried to drive on the lake. But the car fell through the ice and I nearly drowned and froze to death. The deputies shot their rifles across the lake when I came up and hit me three good ones. That's when I crawled up on the bank and fell down the hill. And that's also when the bear came to me, I don't know, maybe in a dream, maybe for real, maybe just one of his cousins.

"How'd you keep from freezing to death? Everybody else would've gotten hypothermia."

A different make-up. I can stand lots of cold. We got it from the Great Grandfather, the first, who was on the Arctic, escaping the Doctor. It's a long story.

Old Roy banked the wood stove and the cabin got warm.

He said if he packed it just right it would last all night. Like a little kid, he sat in front of the fire watching the flames through the glass door. His face got bright red and he sang and hummed and crossed and uncrossed his legs while he carved a piece of wood. I read a Western novel I'd found, maybe one I'd read before, about a rancher hired by the stagecoach line to put a bad guy on the train to justice.

My eyes began to flutter and I drifted off about the time the bad guy's men came to rescue him on the stagecoach. Old Roy climbed into his bed with all of his clothes on and when I looked at him kind of strange, he said, "Habit." I turned toward the wall and watched Poletta come down the stairs wet and naked. She was wearing part of her queen of hearts costume, the little skirt, and the red against her wet black skin looked really, really nice and turned me on.

In the middle of the night I felt my chest tightening and I couldn't move my legs. At first I thought I was having a heart attack. As I struggled to wake, the cop roughed me up and pushed my face. But the cop turned out not to be the cop.

What the hell are you doing? I said waking. It was old Roy and he was in bed next to me. He had his arms around me tight and his pants unbuckled.

Get your ass out of here and go sleep in the snow, I said. What the hell's wrong with you? I gave him a shove and he landed hard on the floor.

"Sorry, Francis, sorry," he said. "I get lonely at night. Don't make me sleep outside."

Ah, shit, you goddamn old son of a bitch. You ruined a perfectly good dream about Poletta. And it must have been when you put your arms around me that the cop pushed my chest.

"Did the cop push your chest in real life?"

Nah, not then, not that night, but plenty of times before, and in jail too.

"I've never been in jail before," old Roy said. "I've never even had a parking ticket."

How'd you manage that? What have you been doing all your life?

"Eighty-five years of getting by. I've never owned a house, been a while since I owned a car, and had just one girlfriend."

Who was the girlfriend?

"My cousin Zena."

How old were you?

"It was so long ago, but I can still see Zena's face, or maybe I'm making it up. I was 15, she was 17. Seventy years ago, can you believe it?"

Were you in love?

"'Not with Roy,' her parents said. 'Don't bring that sombuck around, he's your cousin.' I loved her. The uncles didn't like each other, my father and his brothers. She was mature, and pretty, with round boobs, and she liked me, she loved me, a short boy with big ears and not much in the way of talent."

You never had a family or children?

"Never."

What happened with Zena?

"She went away and I never heard much from her, but I wrote her letters, up to a point, when I got her address. She went to college where she was in Oregon, with one of our aunts, the one who really didn't like me. Got married and had a daughter. And there was something else."

What?

"I can't say."

Hmmm, why not?

"Can't say."

Then why bring it up?

"There was a whole something else."

What kind of something else?

141

"There was . . . somebody else."

Ever had a dog? I asked, thinking about what he meant by "somebody else."

"One with bad teeth and hair, Tuffy. Nineteen years and he could barely walk at the end. Shit everywhere. But I loved that little dog."

Roy got back in his bed and I fell asleep, but kept waking, hearing scratching and Roy's talk-breathing dreams and him licking his lips. Then I woke once and thought for a long time about old Roy, what a strange life he'd had and that at 85 there seemed to be a big chunk missing. Why didn't he go after cousin Zena, and where was she today? Hopefully she was surrounded by great grandchildren, or maybe at 87 she was dead. And here was Roy's sad life of sleeping in empty cabins, eating bad food, making a few bucks here and there, living all alone.

But as I thought about him, I also thought how my life wasn't much different. I wanted to change it, do it another way, not have so much trouble, be able to trust, not continue the way of the Grandfathers. But I wasn't sure how to do that.

When the first of the dreams arrived, the ones that came like scatter shots, they involved the police: being in the back of a car with the siren on, handcuffed, banging and slamming. Then running and running through deep snow, out of breath, my nostrils burning, freezing. And old Roy standing on the road pointing at the cabin so the police would know where I was.

But we settled into a rhythm for six weeks, me in training and Roy with a big cut-down project of beetle kill in the national forest. And no police, or anyone else for that matter, showed up.

We'd get home, cook something real quick like pasta with tuna or little weenies, clean the dishes, then we'd put the milk crates out and sit and talk and smoke some of Roy's roll-it-up tobacco sprinkled with weed. Seemed like Roy had worked everywhere and mostly shit jobs, or so he said: packing house, railroad, steel mill, sewage plant. I wasn't sure he was telling the truth about some of the details, but I liked to listen. And Roy didn't mind so much that I didn't share where I'd been and what I'd done.

He also liked to talk about the day's work and what happened when the tree he was cutting twisted and almost hit the hippie kid on the crew who wandered around high. His stories came with gestures or demonstrations, and he would get up from our little table if we were inside and march around to demonstrate how the fuck-head boss acted on the beetle-cut crew, or how one of the guys liked to secretly steal things out of other people's lunches and eat them. I couldn't imagine, though, what an 85-year-old senior citizen did on tree-cutting crews.

In the smoke-jumper training we started off every morning with sit-ups and push-ups, running, then we'd work with parachutes, climbing trees, CPR and first-aid, reading maps, safe ways to use a chainsaw, and mock airplane exits. We did this for the first two weeks of that part. And then the next Monday we were going to start our first practice jumps. I was anxious to tell old Roy about it and hoped he wouldn't monopolize the conversation, which he had a tendency to do.

The van dropped me off at the road in front of the cabin and as I walked down the trail I felt a wave of, I don't know what, like joy or something. The sheriff hadn't picked me up or even come close to arresting me, but I also kept my head down and let Roy do the grocery shopping. And the training and work were going pretty well, real well, and the other trainees and the leaders turned out to be good people. They even gave us phones, little cheapies but they were phones, with minutes on them. And the most important part is they

143

didn't know one thing about my past. Or didn't act like they did.

There was another guy too, a Navajo guy, real quiet, that was almost as tall as me, six-seven, and we were starting to become friends, Nils Naize. He was pretty good at doing everything, like stuffing the packs and getting all the supplies for the overnighters. Only thing is he ate too much Spam. I don't know if that was a Nils thing or a Navajo thing. Plus I could feel myself getting fitter and I was tossing some of my anger. Something told me Nils knew about the Denver trouble, the way he looked at me and nodded his head.

As I got closer to the cabin that day, I could see that the front door and the screen door were both open, wide open, and my first thought was that the bear had paid us a visit. I turned off into the trees and circled around to the far side of the cabin, by the outhouse, just in case it was either the bear, or the other kind of bear. Then I thought there might've been somebody inside, going through our stuff and I wanted to rush the place and rip them up. But there was no movement, no sound. I took a chance and walked carefully up to the back door.

And there he was. Groceries spilled on the floor. Legs sprawled in different directions. Blood on his head from where he'd hit it on the table. I called to him from the door; no answer. I went in and checked his pulse. Nothing. Roy was dead in the kitchen. Had been for a while, too, maybe all day, maybe just since lunch. I tried to give him CPR but nothing started up again, not his heart and not his breathing. I wished I had the defib machine.

I picked him up and put him on his bunk. Old Roy seemed to shrivel in front of me. He got small on the blanket. I took off his boots and jacket.

As I was looking at him I reached up and touched his beard, like a straw broom or a horse's tail, and then his face, his chest, his belly and his legs. I was going to touch his crotch, too, but I thought he might wake up smiling.

I sat in Roy's chair at the little table and wondered what to do. My guess, incidentally, was that he died of a bad heart attack. Sudden, boom, and then he was on the ground. Probably didn't know what hit him, judging by the way the groceries were spread out on the floor.

What I was thinking about was this: If I called 9-1-1 the EMTs would come and the sheriff would do the follow-up, or the sheriff would come first, lead the way into the cabin and ask me all kinds of questions, want to see my I.D. Maybe I should just leave and not come back, go to Denver and hide out again. But then the fire job would be over and I'd be on the run again, and I liked working in the mountains. I switched the radio on and off, on and off, checked the phone, went to the outhouse, busted up a few blocks of wood, and sat on a milk crate out front.

I figured it came down to only two things: take him someplace and leave him, then send some kind of anonymous tip to the cops, telling them I'd seen somebody alongside a trail, or even behind a store, which I didn't much like the idea of doing. Or I could wrap him up in his blanket, take him to a nice place alongside a stream, and give him a good burial.

With climbing rope that was in the cabin, I cinched Roy up on my back facing out. I couldn't take the trail to the stream, the shortcut, because what if somebody came along and saw me with a dead man strapped to my back. Hey, Mr. Sheriff, there's a weird dude on the trail lugging a dead guy around. No, he didn't look to be carrying a weapon. He was big, though, maybe eight, nine feet. Strange.

There was a place Roy liked to go where he made a campfire once and cooked us some trout on sticks and potatoes in foil. The ground might have been softer because the stream was just thirty feet away, but then there were the tree roots.

I propped old Roy up against a spruce, and with the shovel began to dig.

I tried not to think of myself during this time, out of respect, but it was hard. Off to the west was the sound of moving water and it was so lovely. Roy told me once that he liked to take baths in that stream, cold as it was, and he'd gotten so that he preferred it, even if there was hot water. He liked to wash his underwear right on himself, socks too, with a bar of soap. In some ways Roy was a modest guy. And he was a quirky guy. Liked to hum unrecognizable music, too.

I wanted to mention to him once that the jokes he was telling were dumb and came straight out of *Boys' Life*, the Boy Scout magazine, or somewhere like that. Why did the man salute the refrigerator? Because it was a General Electric. But he kept on. And when he got tickled, he shifted to this little titter of a laugh, kind of under his breath and against his teeth, like a Boy Scout might. Being a Boy Scout probably was the highlight of his life, or maybe wanting to be one was. When I went through his pockets he had a wad of Boy Scout pins and military badges inside, and I could see he'd been rubbing them like good-luck charms.

After I was done digging, I unwrapped the blanket enough to show his face. I wanted to put something over his eyes and I took two badges that looked alike and stuck them there. Old Roy, I said, anything you want me to know or advise me about before I finish wrapping you up and put you in the ground?

He never gave me advice before so why did I think he would start that day from the grave. But I heard his scratchy voice, maybe just my voice, say stay with the smoke jumpers, they like you. You'll stay out of trouble that way. Anything else? I asked him, or me. I watched to see if his lips moved but they never did. And there will come a time in the hot forest,

Francis. What? What about the hot forest? I asked, and then waited. But nothing more came.

There will come a time in the hot forest, I said to myself a couple of times. Hard to say if he meant in the middle of the day, in August, or something else. I bundled old Roy up again and sat next to him. Birds passed overhead, mostly little cheepers that I didn't recognize, and there was the sound of a bigger creature, maybe a deer, off somewhere, but nothing else.

All right Roy, I said, it's time.

Good to meet you, Francis. See you later, refrigerator.

With that I set him in the ground and began covering him up. I threw the dirt in gently, all around him, asked him if he was ok, and then filled in the rest. But I didn't want to leave him there. And I felt weird going back to the cabin alone, without Roy.

That night I had a dream, like a cartoon, of a fox or something, a badger, digging up Roy's grave and Roy rising up, saying hey, son of bitch, and chasing the critter off. It was a quick cartoon, or so it seemed, and in the morning the sheet was untucked and wrapped around my neck. Roy waved to me and smiled at me with big teeth, then pulled the dirt back over him, like a blanket.

14.

Two things happened. Actually, three. One, a girl who was working for the Forest Service came to stay at the cabin. Two, when I was in a Pakistani convenience store, I saw Pindar on TV with Hennie right next to him. And three, I found $650 in Roy's duffel bag at the very bottom when I reached in and did a quick search. It was in a little plastic envelope with a zipper, and there was a tiny slip of paper with an incomplete address in Oregon and the name Anez, no last name. I didn't especially need it, and I wasn't sure about the address, so I just put it in my back pocket. When I got near a post office I'd find the missing zip code and mail it to Anez.

The Forest Service girl was named Opal and she was from a women's college back east, doing a summer internship helping out in timber auctions. She had big freckles, bright red hair, and was about five feet tall. She also cussed and swaggered like a man.

"I'll take the fucking bed by the stove," she said the afternoon she arrived.

That's old Roy's bunk, I said, take a different one. I didn't have any idea I was going to say that or that I thought that way.

"Where's this fucking Roy?" she demanded.

He'll be back tomorrow or the next day, I said.

"How about this fucking top bunk in the back?" she barked. "Roy doesn't own this motherfucker, does he?"

It's open, I said. There were four metal, government-issue bunk beds.

"How the hell you fit in that goddamn bed, as tall as you are?"

It's a problem but I get by, I said. You can stow your gear under the bottom bunk, that should be ok.

"No shit, Sherlock. And just thought I'd let you know that sometimes my fucking boyfriend might stop by, stay the night. You got a problem with that?"

Yeah, I do. It's against the rules. No overnight visiting.

No idea where I came up with that, but she didn't question it. I also wanted to say And that's Roy's chair, and his woodpile, and his oatmeal. But I held back.

That night the boyfriend came by on his mountain bike.

"Terp," he said when I asked his name. He didn't bother to ask me mine. And "You're a big motherfucker, ain't you?"

Terp was the male counterpart to Opal. Short, with wiry hair and milk-white skin, and a cowboy kind of walk.

"Don't say nothing about my fucking name, neither."

Why would I want to do that? I said.

"Lotta people think I say Twerp, not Terp, which is short for Terrapin, and I've gotten into it over that."

I'll try and remember that.

"Where the fuck you work?" Terp asked.

"He's a fucking fire guy," Opal said butting in.

I work as a fucking smoke jumper. I almost laughed when I added "fucking" to smoke jumper.

"Most of the smoke jumpers I've met are fucking jerks."

You've met a few, then? I asked.

"Gotten into it with a couple of the pricks," he said.

Sorry to hear that. Most of the ones I've met are nice guys.

"I might be here late visiting Opal," he said. "You don't have a fucking problem with that, do you?"

Yeah, actually I do, I said. Curfew's at nine, Forestry rule. Which again was something made up.

"That curfew's for fucking kids."

I'm a big kid, I said. I have to get up early while we're in training.

"Ok," Terp said. "Week days nine. Weekends late."

This is going to be hard, I thought. Terp was a fucking twerp, as was Opal, a twerpette, and they were always necking on the beds, especially Roy's bed, laughing loud, and cussing.

"Where's this fucking Roy guy?" Opal demanded after Roy had not shown his face for a couple days.

He's camping out, I said, catching fish, probably by a river somewhere. I tried to stay out of the cabin as much as I could, sat outside a lot, and finished the Western.

"Whatcha fucking reading?" Terp said pointing while I was still reading the book.

A new version of an old west story, I said.

"Cowboys and fucking Injuns," he said snarling.

Terp, I said, and felt like slapping his puffy pink lips, but turned away and went for a hike. When I returned to the cabin to start dinner, they were in the middle of getting it on.

"Maybe somebody better knock next time they fucking come in all of sudden."

Maybe it's time for you two to take a stroll.

"You saying I gotta fucking leave," Terp said in my face.

It would be good if you took a break while I made some dinner, I said, and felt like lifting the little shit by the neck in the air.

I'd found a book in Roy's bag, *Amazing True Facts from Around the World*, and started reading it. The hottest temperature ever recorded. The longest distance traveled on a gallon can of gas. The woman who gave birth to the most children. The kids were outside arguing in the dark. At one point I could hear Terp slap Opal, and then Opal crying.

"What?" he said to me when I stood looking out the screen door and then stepped onto the porch. "She fucking deserved it, the little cunt. And you don't scare me none."

Opal was curled up in a ball at Terp's feet.

"Goddamnit to fucking hell, quit that crying," Terp said and kicked the bottom of her shoes. "I hate crying."

When I took a step closer, he picked up his bike - they'd both ridden them to the cabin that day, thrown them in the yard - and said, "You fucking coming or you just going to lay there?" Then he flipped me off.

Opal covered her face with her hands and curled up into an even tighter ball.

"Bitch," Terp shouted and rode away quickly.

Inside I made some of Roy's famous tomato soup from the can, with a couple of spoonfuls of salsa, a few shakes of parmesan, and a whole package of chopped up hot dogs.

Before too long Opal came in and asked what kind of soup that was.

Tomato, I said, and she asked if there was enough fucking soup for her.

"What's these fucking floaty things in here?" she asked sniffing and wiping her eyes.

Hot dogs, I said.

"I'm a vegetarian," she said.

Well, that's all we've got for dinner, I said, except macaroni, which would take a while to fix.

"Oh, hell," Opal said, "I guess I could just eat them or pick them out."

I'm making some toast to go with the soup too.

"Great," Opal said in a soft voice, "I love toast with soup."

Opal sat at the kitchen table, in Roy's chair, and daydreamed while I buttered the toast. She slurped her soup and absently blew on every spoonful, then began to whimper.

"Terp is really kind of an asshole, you know. I'm not even sure why I hang out with him."

Yeah, I said, holding back saying anything. How long have you been seeing him?

"Six months, maybe. We met at the phone store. It was right when I got here and I was looking for a western kind of guy, which I thought he was."

This is Roy's recipe, incidentally. This was the way he made tomato soup.

"I'm beginning to think this Roy person isn't ever fucking coming back."

What makes you say that?

"Well, I've been here three days and he hasn't shown up yet."

Old Roy is buried over by the creek, near where he liked to fish and have a campfire.

"You mean just in the ground."

No, he was wrapped in his favorite blanket.

"Didn't he have family or anything to look after him?"

His wife Zena was killed in a tragic accident in Oregon, they'd traveled the world, and he never remarried.

"How old was this fucking Roy?"

He was 85 and he was still out there every day in the woods cutting down trees with a crew. I used to ask him, Is today the day, meaning his last day, especially when he got up slow in the morning, and he would say Maybe tomorrow.

"That's actually what I do, my internship," Opal said, "work with fucking contractors cutting down trees affected by pine beetles. But I've never seen this Roy."

After we'd finished dinner, such as it was, and Opal had allowed me to wash the dishes, we sat outside and smoked one of Roy's cigarettes with a little weed in it. She got real talkative and explained the mystery of a number of things, like how GMOs spell the end of human civilization, why cell phones cause prostate cancer, and where missing messages go from communications satellites. While we were sitting on the milk crates, Opal fell asleep and slumped over. I took that opportunity to change into my pajama shorts and start reading again.

"What? Were you just going to fucking leave me out there all night?" Opal demanded when she finally woke and came in.

No, I said, I would have put a blanket over you.

"Goddamnit," she said slapping the mattress on her bed.

She went to the outhouse and when she came back stripped to her underwear and got under the covers. She hung her little bra on the metal bedpost and began singing along to a song coming out of her phone into her earbuds.

"Don't even fucking think about coming up here," she said in an off-handed way.

I'll try not to, I said. You ready for the light to be off?

"I'll switch it off in a few minutes," she said, and added. "I can't fucking believe that guy Terp."

Two hours later I got up and switched it off when she'd fallen asleep.

The next night and until she left, Opal told me stories when we went to bed. All of them just a few sentences long.

"I had a dog once when I was a little girl who could sing and dance when I turned on the stereo. He liked Marvin Gaye a lot, especially his concerts. Brother, brother, brother. We had to get rid of him, though, 'cause he wouldn't leave my step-mother's cat alone. And the new family sold him to a circus for a lot of money."

"Once my friends and I stole a car late at night that was parked at the curb running, and we drove it on the interstate 150 miles an hour. It could have gone a lot faster. The cops couldn't even catch us. And they brought in a helicopter."

It was clear Opal was making the stories up and when she was finished she always asked, "You believe that shit could happen?"

Each time I responded, Yeah, of course that could happen, Opal.

Then one day Opal told me about the sheriff finding Terp next to his bicycle on the side of the road; they figured a car or truck had bumped him and left him. He was dead.

I wanted to say that I knew what happened to Terp, that I'd met him one day on the road, and that he'd called me a shithead and accused me of fucking Opal.

Opal said she was leaving, going back home, that her internship was almost over anyway.

I asked where home was and she said, Connecticut. How you going to get there? I wondered.

"Think I'll take the bus, she said. "You know, I just made all those stories up."

Really? I said, and she said, Really.

"I have this thing about lying," she said. "I like to lie and I can't stop."

Opal got up early with me the morning she left.

"Thanks for not trying to take advantage," she said. "I would've had to get rough. Take care, Francis, and watch those fires."

She hugged me and pressed her small frame against me. Drop me a note when you get there, I said, and she said she would.

Pindar and Hennie were on TV again and the headline said he was considering a run for governor. He introduced Hennie as his fiancé and even held her hand up in the air with his. It listed his occupation as former ranch owner and entrepreneur. They would have a rally in another town in the mountains that weekend.

Pindar and Hennie were on the TV in the Forestry training room and we'd been watching the news early in the morning and then going into the field, sometimes jumping out of planes two or three times a day. It had been hot all over Colorado and the bosses kept telling us to be ready, keep our phones on, we could get called out any time day or night.

I thought about Pindar and Hennie and what was happening there. Those two together, I didn't understand it. And where Pindar was living and how had he survived the ranch fire?

My first forest fire was not much of one. Fifty acres north of Eagle and no smoke jumping required. A little backburning and some suppression with shovels and a dozer and that was it. The air tankers sprayed the containment and we were done in the afternoon. We had to stick around, though, and watch for flame-ups or reignition because it was so close to a city.

"Stay alert," they told us, "never know when the next one will come."

Roger stopped me and asked if I'd seen my friend the bear around the cabin.

Nope, no bears around the cabin, I said.

"How about an old man?" he asked, kind of slipping it in there.

You mean like with a big white Santa beard and about 85 years old? I asked.

"Yeah, that's the guy," he said. "He sleeps in all our cabins and we have to run him off."

Nah, I said, I never saw an old man with a beard like that.

Roger smiled at me and said, "You ever find your I.D?"

I haven't been down to Denver yet, Roger. I'll get it next time I do.

Roger asked if I needed a ride anyplace and I said Breckenridge. That's where Pindar was going to give his speech, at a big white tent in town. I wanted to hear him, but I also wanted to look at him, see how bad he'd been injured.

While I was waiting for them to get started, I dropped Roy's money in the mail to Anez after I got the zip. I wrote her a note telling her that old Roy had died, that I'd buried him by the creek, and that I still had his clothes and books and could send them to her.

When Pindar began I stood on the side, out of the way but close, so I could see him. Hennie was sitting in a chair near him and she applauded at every point in his speech; maybe that was her job. There was probably a hundred people in the crowd, which included the media. Pindar started by welcoming people and telling us that there was nothing more valuable to him than his family, his religion, and his fellow Coloradans.

"I love Colorado and Coloradans," he said, "and I know how important these mountains are to you folks. My family's been in the ranching business for decades and I've been an entrepreneur most of my life, the last time in the humanitarian field of private organ-transplants. I attended college here, was in the National Guard here. And like a lot of you, I've seen fire and I've seen rain and I've seen lonely times I thought would never end."

Hennie clapped and a few people clapped and while Pindar waited to begin again, he saw me standing on the side. With a head movement and a turn, he tried to get his security to look at me and he whispered something to Hennie.

When he faced away from us, I could see the side of his head and neck were scarred and his hands were scarred too. He lost his place in the speech and stumbled, said some things twice, but continued talking, saying how much he valued education, and education . . . education for young struggling mothers, and that he wanted to provide, provide educational help for people who really wanted to, wanted to get ahead.

Hennie hadn't spotted me yet when the phone buzzed and I stepped outside the tent. I could see her through the flap searching and searching. There was a text that gave an all-call for a fire near Kremmling, and that we should meet at a certain pick-up spot as soon as possible, there would be vans.

I wanted to talk to Hennie, she was always my friend, ask about Pindar, ask if she'd been to the ranch, ask where Pindar was living, and if she was really his fiancé. But I didn't have time; we had a fire that needed attention. And I wasn't sure I could trust her now.

The long ride in the dark van gave me a chance to think about Pindar; what a strange man he was, and now running for governor. People sitting around me talked with that nervous energy, I was a little bit nervous, but more about Pindar and Hennie seeing me and sending security out to find me, causing trouble when things had been going so well.

The fire was in danger of getting out of hand, they told us, because there'd been no rain for a year, it was very dry, and it was windy.

If the winds shift, the bosses said, look for an exit, always have an escape route, and use your shelter if you have to. They were talking about the portable fire shelters we were issued in case we got stuck.

Nils had told me that worse than burning up is the danger of big branches falling off trees and hitting you on the head, even with a helmet on. It happened to him on the New Mexico side of the Weminuche. A tree fell and hit him on the shoulder, broke his collarbone, and burned him a little.

"I had to walk five miles out to the vehicle," he said, "and leave the other guys behind. One of them died that day. I should have been there to help him. It took me a while to come back."

We got all our gear ready at the staging area, suited up, and waited for morning. If the fire had been a big one, we would have started at night. It cooled down some about midnight, but the wind came up through the trees, roaring like a jet engine, which was a real bad sign. Spotters reported that it had begun to move fast, shifting, burning ranch houses, killing livestock, and torching equipment.

At three we mobilized. "Let's go to work, men," the bosses said. "We've got some suppressing to do." The fire had become dangerous.

As we got closer we could smell the burn and see the glow in the distance.

"It's coming," the bosses said, "take every precaution."

The air tankers had been dropping retardant but the report said it was blowing all over the place and they couldn't get enough of it directly on the hot spots.

Nils was the leader of our small hand crew and he made sure we had good pulaskis and shovels and chainsaws. He got us new respirators, too. He was our lookout and showed us some shortcuts to establishing a fireline.

"We need to get some chains dug," Nils said, "take care of these combustibles."

Nils talked to us as we worked and told us to watch for animals, not to worry about them attacking, but just to get out of their way. And right after that, deer came running down the hill, followed by porcupines, a badger, and bunnies. When it got hotter, a mountain lion came panting out of the woods looking confused and stopped to growl something to us. He howled in a confused way and then trotted off.

I don't know how hot it got, but you could feel the difference. Nils got a call that said we might have to bail.

Suddenly, though, the fire was all around us, blocking our way.

Nils said something into the radio and then I could see his mouth say "shit," and he told us we had to get the hell out of there.

"Stay close," he said, "follow me."

Should we get the shelters out? I asked Nils.

"Fuck the shelters," he said.

The fire was sucking the oxygen out of the air and it was hard to breathe. It didn't look like there was any way out, but Nils thought he could see a way. He didn't want another repeat. He didn't want this crew to get stuck, get burned up.

We could see somebody on the other side of the fire and he was waving and pointing not to come this way, go around the other way. We saw the clearing he was pointing to and made for it. But just as we got there the top of a tree blew off and a big inferno basket landed right in the way. Part of it must have hit me from behind, on my legs, because one minute I was standing, moving along ok, and the next I was down. I could feel the branches burning me. I could hear Nils calling me, "Francis, Francis," but I couldn't see him. I was pinned down and the fire was all around me.

Shit, I thought, son of a bitch this is hot. And Nils and another guy knocked the branches off me and began to drag me away.

"Can you walk?" he said right into my face so I could hear him.

I didn't know if I could but I said, Yeah, I can walk, and they held onto me and we hiked quickly.

But Nils stumbled on something, a rock it seemed like, maybe a root, we were running hard, and he went down and hit his head full force. It knocked him out and the other guys were already through the hole. It was just the three of us about to roast.

"Put his arm across your shoulder and lift," the other guy, Crosley, said. "We're gonna fucking die if we don't get the hell out of here."

Big as he was and being out like he was made him really heavy. We had to sort of drag-lift him and then right over a bunch of fire and he still didn't come to. Nils's head was cut wide open and he was bleeding like crazy. We made it through and out to the group, jumped over a batch of burning shit, but it wasn't clear Nils would be all right. The superintendent told everybody to get in the van quickly and pointed at somebody to drive. We stretched Nils out on the seat and got the first-aid kit.

"Drive," the superintendent yelled and pressed a patch over Nils's cut to stop the bleeding. "Get on the radio and call in a chopper."

Nils hadn't moved one inch since he'd hit his head, and it looked like he'd knocked a tooth out too. At one point, while we were driving, the fire had jumped across the road and we had to drive right through it.

The superintendent asked how I was doing and I pulled my pant legs up to see. Both legs were burned behind my knees, my skin was raw and bleeding, and my pants were scorched.

There was no room on the chopper or otherwise I would have gone with Nils. The EMTs cut my pants off and started cleaning me up. Third degree for sure.

Was he breathing? I asked the supe. Could you tell if he was breathing?

He paused and shook his head: "No breath, no heartbeat."

15.

A letter came from Anez a week and a half after I'd sent mine.

Hi, Francis, thanks, wow, that money came at exactly the right time. I really needed the 650 for the house and things. Sorry to hear about Roy. I guess he was pretty old though. You guys were working in the forest together, right, and were friends? Funny, I never met Roy, but I heard about him every once in a while and got a birthday card once. He was my grandmother's cousin, and maybe they were, like, boyfriend and girlfriend, unofficially, when they were teenagers. But Grandma's parents wouldn't let them hang around and they sent her away, out here. Maybe he told you all this. And they sort of kept in touch, from what I understand, even though Grandma was married to Grandpa. Or Roy did for a while. I mean, there was a drawer full of them, but they were kind of short actually, with clippings or funny newspaper articles. Even postcards with jokes. But I'm not sure how long Grandma kept up after getting married. Maybe not so much. We didn't know what to do with Roy's things after Grandma died, so we just kept them, wrapped them up and put them in the garage. Roy heard about Grandma dying somehow and sent a card to Mom and me. Mom kinda got upset for some reason, but I didn't think she knew him, aside from the letters. Not sure about that. Guess you can just keep his stuff or give it away. Drop me a note if you feel like it. I have a girl, incidentally. Take care.

Anez

When I did a quick check of Roy's bag, there was a pair of dress shoes, wool and flannel shirts, a white dress shirt, tee shirts, jeans, khakis with the cuffs rolled up, briefs, and socks. He was wearing his hikers and a flannel shirt when I buried him. And tucked down into the side of the bag was a writing tablet with skinny joints stuck in between the pages. But here's something that was pretty curious: The top page of the tablet was blank except for a name, *Royal*. He was about to write somebody by the name of Royal a letter when he died. It actually said, *To my girl, Royal.* No clues about who Royal might be. An old-lady girlfriend, a godchild, somebody in the past.

It took me a few weeks before I could walk right. The scabs turned into scars and the scars tightened up. It was kind of ugly and spongey looking. I had to do office work for a while, then I could rejoin the crew. We had a ceremony for Nils after the fire got put out. Nobody else was injured or killed. Nils's brother was the only one of his family who came and he took him back home in an S.U.V. to the reservation outside Window Rock. Big guy like he was, he really smacked his head and lost a lot of blood. Somebody else on the crew said he had a tumor on his eye nerve, that he'd been having a hard time seeing out of the left eye, that he'd been getting treatment for it, and that that might have had something to do with it too.

We had a couple more fires, and some controlled burns, before I was completely healed, but I went along with the crew anyway. One was in Utah, out of our territory, and the other was over by Grand Junction, south of there, in the Uncompahgre. But here's the thing: I got nervous whenever we got near a fire, real nervous. I didn't want to get too close. They assigned me van duty, driving, but I helped the guys with their equipment and repacking their chutes and getting ready. I was really looking forward to floating down into the forest with a parachute, but it wasn't going to happen for a while, maybe not ever.

Roger kept after me about my I.D., and the bear, and I considered going into Denver to get it, but put him off. At one point, I thought it might be all right to go back into the city, that things would probably have blown over, that the cops would have given up looking for me, but maybe not. And then my life would be finished if they found me. For killing a cop you go to jail forever. No chance of parole. And they would pin Poletta's murder on me to ensure I stayed gone.

Here's the thing about the bear: I did sense he was circling the cabin, wandering around at night, maybe sleeping outside in the bushes part of the time. I never saw him, I thought I heard him, and the bushes were flattened around us.

I say us because the cabin was full. Four people getting into each other's ways, breathing through their mouths at night, talking in their sleep, pissing all over the outhouse. One girl, three of us dudes.

The girl was named Gail, but she acted more like an Emily. Gail-Emily wasn't a cusser like Opal, but she wasn't much of a talker either. And she liked to have things done her way. Like having the sink perfectly clean before fixing her own dinner, and she never invited anyone to share. Lots of cabbage and carrots, which smelled and didn't interest me anyway. She was a cabbage salad eater.

She was also the first one to notice the bear. The other two guys were clueless. Gail-Emily actually worked for the Forest Service, unlike Opal, who was just an intern. She was in personnel and passed messages over from their office, mostly about my I.D.

"There's somebody out there," Gail-Emily said one night. "There's somebody watching the cabin."

I started to say Oh, no, it's not a peeping Tom, it's just a bear, but then I thought she might run out screaming.

I don't think so, I said. Probably just a type of noisy little critter.

"Do you have a gun of some kind?"

They don't allow guns in the Forestry cabins, I said. Which was a lie.

"What if we're being stalked, and then they attack us?" she said.

Who would be the theys, I asked, attacked by who?

Gail-Emily was a tight-looking girl with short hair, on the thin side, and kind of nervous, especially around the two clunky guys.

"What about those wilderness kind of people with automatic weapons?"

Yes, what about them? There's not much we could do if they came around. She'd suggested we lock everything up.

The two guys ate power bars and ketchup sandwiches, tucked themselves away whenever they could and read sci-fi comics.

After we'd turned out the lights and things settled down, I could hear the bear crunching around outside. I knew Gail-Emily's finely tuned ears would hear him too, and she breathed maybe a sigh, swallowed hard, and then pulled the covers over her head.

With the windows open, the bear put his nose against the screen and took in the cabin air. He kind of moaned through the window and sounded like he had something on his mind.

Ok, bear, I said, after listening a while, and got up out of bed and put my flip-flops on. From Gail-Emily's bunk I could hear a small, protective squeak. I thought by getting up I would offer myself as a sacrifice and at least keep him from eating the whole group.

The bear at first approached me and stood up. I was much taller, but he was heavier, like a wrestler. I stood still so he could sniff me, and he said something like arrhh-ungghh, or unhhgg-ehh, or both. He had a big raspy tongue and he licked each of my legs.

Let us walk, you and I, I said, a touch nervous. It was dark and there was a bear next to me, and I thought they might find me in the woods, legs half-eaten, no I.D., a full-bellied bear sitting next to what was left of me, and then someone, the sheriff might say, Isn't that the killer, the guy we were after, the one we were chasing? Looks like the bear took care of him for us.

But he didn't eat me. Or scratch me. Or bite me. He seemed like he just wanted to walk on the trail next to me and growl kind of low. Could've been he was hungry and couldn't find any berries or roots, or maybe somebody had run him off from somewhere—the sheriff by a Dumpster, or maybe he was looking for a little bear love, a girlfriend, a piece of ass.

The moon came up over the pines, and the bear sat and looked up at the sky, and I sat and looked up at the same sky.

We walked on to the stream where I'd buried old Roy, and the bear scratched at his grave. There were already claw marks, but it didn't seem as if he was trying to dig him up.

That's Roy's grave, I said to the bear. And the bear said something back.

We sloshed across the stream and walked on a-ways. I thought maybe the bear wanted me to see his hideout, and before long we were at a rock lean-to that if you weren't looking you might not see. He led me to the front and then I could see what the problem was: Someone had started a campfire and trashed the place up with beer bottles and paper plates and cans.

The bear made a sad gesture and groaned as if to say "See what I have to put up with."

Yes, bear, I see, I said. Sorry about that. And then I began to clean up the area as he looked away.

Out of the corner of my eye I could see him slumping by one of the rocks. I wanted to reach out and touch him, pat him, but then I thought he might take it wrong or that it might startle him, upset him.

Ok, bear, I said after I'd cleaned up. I better be going.

The bear shook his head but said nothing, and I could see he was watching me. I walked slowly through the forest, partially because I was enjoying the night, and partially in case the bear wandered down the trail looking for me.

When I was halfway home I heard his loud growl and what sounded like pounding and branches breaking.

In the morning, Gail-Emily was the first to get up, just after sunrise. She put her really fancy slippers on and tiptoed around the cabin holding her crotch. She looked out the windows and opened the front and back doors watching for the bear. When she didn't see him she rushed to the outhouse to do her business.

"Did you go out last night?" she asked me when she got back.

Yes, I told her, I did. I wanted a walk in the moonlight, and I couldn't sleep.

"You weren't afraid of something . . . something happening?"

A little, I said, but not too. It was a nice night and the moon was almost full.

"I couldn't tell if I was dreaming or there really was a bear outside."

And what do you think?

"The bushes are all matted down next to the cabin. I wonder if he's been sleeping here."

That could be the deer. Sometimes they come late at night and bed down.

"I've never seen any deer. But I thought I heard the bear last night and on other nights. We better lock up as soon as it gets dark and close the windows."

The two guys were in the habit of jumping up at the last second, cleaning up a little bit and running out the door. That day they did the same thing. Temp computer work for the Forestry admin office, that's what they said they were doing.

I started late because it was the morning I had to go for my clearance physical to see if I could rejoin the crew. I wanted to wait another week, mostly because I was still a little shaky. Dr. Joan looked at my legs and checked me over pretty good. She also checked the bullet wounds.

"You nervous?" she asked.

Oh, I said stretching it out, well. . . .

"Lots of guys are worried when they first go back," she said. "You won't be the first."

Any way that I could extend the time, you know . . . ?

"You'll be all right," she said. "Keep using the cream. Keep all the scars clean. Anything opens up, come and see me."

When I got back to the crew they all clapped and the supe asked if I was ready to fly.

Is that what we're doing today, parachuting? I asked. I didn't want to parachute. I wanted it to be a glide day, drink lattes and eat biscottis. But that wasn't going to happen.

The supe asked me on the side if I was good to go and I said I was. He told me to splash cold water on my face and then get my gear ready. In the mirror in the bathroom I could see what he was talking about: I was white as underwear.

In a few minutes, we were at the landing strip loading our packs into the plane. I made the group wait when I had a bad feeling and repacked my chute. There were just six of us in the big Neptune.

"You ready, Francis?" the guys on either side of me asked.

I held both thumbs up and felt like shitting my pants.

It was beautiful looking out the door, though, the tree-tops, the mossy rock faces, the high lakes, the drainages. And then it was my turn. Click, click, click, click and I was gone.

Earlier, on one of my first jumps, a hawk sidled up on my left and turned to look at me. He had something in his claws, a mouse or a vole or maybe a baby bird, and it, too, turned to look at me, it was alive. This was while I was still in the float. It was just a few seconds. And they were gone.

Pull, I said to myself that morning when I went back, but I was frozen.

Pull, Francis, pull, I said looking at the ground rising quickly.

Pull the fucking goddamn cord, Francis, and then the cloud was out.

I'd kicked it.

On Friday I got a lift to the market and caught the bus part way back to the cabin. Soup, oatmeal, crackers, wieners, noodles, juice, milk, fruit, bread. Something else on the list I couldn't read. And then there was a tap. She'd been watching me without saying anything. She had her arms crossed and we were in the peanut butter aisle, the missing item. She was still as beautiful as I'd remembered her.

"He's afraid of you and wants to meet someplace, Big Boy," Hennie said, "face to face."

Meet for what? I asked.

"To get the air cleared between you, so there's no problem when he becomes governor."

He tried to kill me, take my heart and my blood, maybe I should tell people about that.

"Pindar is worried you'll try something again."

He's a killer, I said. He and his friends were ready to cut me open. It's me that has to worry about him.

"Can you meet him? Do you have a car? Where are you living now?"

Meet where? I asked, shaking my head.

"There's a little ski resort down the highway, up the mountain. Do you think you can find it? Six on Saturday."

I can't make it, I said. I have a bear to meet.

"He can make it worth your while."

I saw his hands and face when I was in the tent, I said. Looked like the fire got him.

"He was lucky to make it out alive. You almost killed him."

That's the story he told you? And where do you come into all this, Hennie? What's your connection?

"People make things attractive, Francis, sometimes it's hard to turn them down. I couldn't work at the club forever. Will you be there, will you meet him?"

Maybe. We'll see. I don't really have anything to gain, do I, aside from the money?

"It could be worth more than the money. Maybe you could get some type of clemency for killing that cop and the black girl."

I could feel my anger rising. I didn't want to meet fucking Pindar and I wanted to get the hell away from Hennie.

I didn't kill that black girl. And I didn't have a choice with the cop.

"Talk to Pindar about it. Maybe he can arrange it now. A phone call to the police chief, at least, with him mediating. Some kind of clemency. How does that sound?"

Where did he get a new heart? I asked Hennie. He must have gotten a heart from somebody.

"He found one," is all Hennie would say, and then she walked away.

I paid for my groceries and caught the bus. I was afraid Pindar's people would follow me and went in and out of stores first. While I was waiting to get on the bus again, I saw the clunky guys in their car and asked if I could get a ride. As we drove they didn't talk much, but instead they made spastic air guitar movements. When they did speak they talked to each other in that sci-fi lingo about parallel universes, extraterrestrials and time travel. I watched out the side windows and in front and behind, and was sure one of Pindar's people was there tailing me. But at the cabin I walked back out to the road and no one was around.

The next day I asked one of the clunky guys if I could borrow his car for a couple hours and promised to fill it with gas. "Dude" was all he said and handed me the keys. I'd decided it would be at least interesting to see Pindar up close and talk to him, tell him what an asshole he was.

I tried to rehearse questions that I might say or things I wanted to talk about, but the two things I wondered about most were how did he avoid getting burned to death, and where did he get the new heart. Plus, where the hell did he get the idea to become governor anyway?

The ski resort was empty and the lifts looked more like electrical power lines that reached over the mountain. I got there early enough to be able to walk around, even sit on one of the chairs still hanging from a cable. It was a lonely place, even though it was beautiful.

Pictures of the ranch and the cattle and the railroad came

to me as I swung in the lift chair. But how I ended up at Pindar's place and why I stayed puzzled me. As I drifted I could hear the sound of crashing, the squeal of brakes, and the feeling of heat on my face.

Down below, on the dirt road, a vehicle approached, but they couldn't see me. It was a big SUV with tinted windows, white, and the door opened just enough to be able to roll something under the car, I could see that far. The vehicle turned around and stopped a few hundred yards down the road. They seemed to be waiting, maybe for me to return or sit up in the car, and then the bomb exploded and the car scattered everywhere and erupted into a ball of flames.

16.

Roger came to the cabin in the morning and gave me a ride to the office. I thought there was some problem because he never came out to see me. He looked around at the four bunks and said they were going to have to go after my friend.

Which friend is that? I asked, afraid he might be referring to somebody from Denver who'd moved to the mountains, or even one of Pindar's people.

"The bear mauled a couple people," he said. "Three to be exact. Eyewitnesses, and he seemed to go after one of them in particular. Tore him all up. They're not sure he's going to make it."

Where did this happen? I asked.

"Not far from here," Roger said. "On the other side of the creek. They were sitting around a campfire and maybe the bear was after something and one of the campers wouldn't let him have it."

Or maybe that was the bear's spot, maybe that's where he lived. They were trespassing. Was it right next to some rocks?

"I haven't been to the spot yet, but they had a hell of a time getting emergency in there. Guy nearly bled to death. Bear almost ripped his arm off when he swatted him, according to the other people."

What happened to the bear? I asked.

"Apparently they were able to run him off, but nobody's spotted him since or heard any reports about him. There's no relocating bears like this. When they go after people we have to put them down."

I'd have to go out and search for him that night, tell him he had to get the hell away, if he was even around, if they hadn't found him and killed him yet.

And then there was what to tell my clunky roommate who loaned me his car what happened.

Straight up: Some guys in a white SUV rolled a bomb under your car and destroyed it.

"What? Did you wreck it?" he asked. "Did you have an accident? You didn't wreck it, did you?"

No, really, I said, somebody tossed something under your car and it exploded, caught fire.

"Show me," he said. "Where is it?"

They hauled it off after the fire department came and put it out. There were parts everywhere.

"You're kidding, right? Where's my car, dude? Give me the keys."

I gave him the keys and he hurried outside. He came in just as quickly. He was crying.

"Dude," he said shaking all over, "that's not even my car. It was my girlfriend's. She's in India now. She left it here and will be back pretty soon. She's going to be really upset. It was new, her parents gave it to her for graduation."

I thought if I'd said something about extraterrestrials coming and absconding with it he might be ok with that.

Sorry, I said, I'm not kidding, man.

"Did they give you a ticket or something? At least I could show her that."

I didn't want to get into trouble, I said. This was at the little ski resort. I was supposed to meet somebody and I was afraid of what might happen if I said the car was mine. I had to hide when they came. There were cops and fire.

"Shit," he said. "Shit, shit."

Sorry, I said. I'm really sorry.

"You didn't sell it, did you?" he asked.

No, I didn't sell it.

"Did somebody steal it? Go ahead and tell me if someone stole it when you left it unlocked. That can happen."

Nobody stole it. I wish they had.

"Who would want to put a bomb under the car? Why would they do that? Are you in some kind of trouble? Do you owe money?"

No, I don't owe any money, I said. I don't know who blew up your girlfriend's car. Which was a lie. It was Pindar or his people who were trying to kill me, or send me a message, as paybacks.

The clunky guys moved out the next day, Sunday, and I began tracking Pindar's appearances everywhere he went. Denver, Colorado Springs, Pueblo, Boulder, Fort Collins, Greeley. Christian schools, small manufacturing companies, coffee shops. *The Fire and Rain Campaign*, he called it. "Uniting for families, for all of us" was his slogan. "And we've had threats to the campaign, to my life, to my fiancé Hennie's life. We've had to step up security in an unprecedented way. But we'll survive. We'll become even stronger. Stronger for all of you. For working Coloradans. And for those Front Range folks, Western Slope folks, San Luis Valley folks, Durango folks, Eastern Plains folks, people who want to make it better for the next generation, who want to build things, not tear things down."

This was the gist of his different talks that had been printed. I'd heard him enough times on the radio, on TV, on the internet. And whenever I got a chance, and he was in a nearby town, I began disguising myself and going to hear him talk. But what do you do when you're six-nine and stand out in any crowd. A wheelchair is a great prop. So is a stocking cap and sunglasses. Even Hennie didn't recognize me.

I came close enough to shake his hand a couple times.

One day, I said, one day.

For two nights I went out walking, looking for the bear, and I almost gave up. Then on the second night he was there. They'd already started looking for him. He was not at the rocks, but off somewhere where I could hear him. He was following me, but at a distance, where I couldn't quite see him. Grousing, that's what it sounded like he was doing, like the old men who grumble-talk, talking under his breath, swearing in bear lingo.

What did you fucking expect? I shouted out to him. You can't just go ripping people's arms off and not expect anything to happen. They're coming to get you, bear, probably starting big time tomorrow morning, so you better be gone. Forget about hideouts or caves. Move to another state, a completely different forest. And get rid of that tag in your ear.

He waited and I waited. He said something that sounded like a cross between complaining and crying. Then he moved off, slowly, reluctantly, and before too long I couldn't hear him at all.

In the morning the professional hunters with dogs came past the cabin on ATVs. Someone had spotted a bear nearby, they said.

"What's all this about?" Gail-Emily asked. "Looks like they're going after an escaped convict"

I don't think so, I said, but maybe something escaped and they're going after it.

A couple weeks went by and a letter came again. I'd written one to Anez, in response to hers, something short, how're things, hope the house is ok, that kind of B.S. And there was a picture in the envelope of her with someone, a child. "N @ 9" it said on the back. I held it closer to see what Anez actually looked like. Glasses, a nice nose, wavy hair, something in the front, and her arm around "N." Not bad looking. Tallish.

She just started right up like we were old friends.

That little girl in the picture is Neza, my daughter, Zena's great granddaughter. She's a special girl in a lot of ways. Kind of small for her age, I know, especially when you look at her dad and I, but she's really smart. We almost lost her a couple yrs ago. She's got something like a blood disorder. Not exactly but similar.

Hi, Francis. Sorry, forgot to say that. I'm going for a job interview later this morning. To bring in money I have people rent rooms, mostly international students, girls from the Philippines in the nanny program, but it's not consistent. It's a really big house, it was Royal's, my mother's, before she got an apartment. Some months it's good money, some months nothing. The job is at a leasing office in a senior's building, front desk, half time, which is all I need.

Where we are we get a lot of salmon and Grandpa showed me how to smoke it. That's another thing I do. If you like smoked salmon I could send you some, a mix maybe. There's honey smoked, one with a spicy rub, and one with a smoked pinyon flavor.

Wish me luck today and maybe we can talk again. Thanks for your letter too.

Take care,
Anez

Good luck, I said out loud, but to nobody. Hope you get it.
. . . it was Royal's, my mother's.
I stood holding the letter. If I hadn't been paying attention I might have missed it. Royal. That was Anez's mother, Zena's daughter. Which, after thinking about it, with that name, could make her old Roy's child. They'd had a baby, I was sure of it. She was sent away to Oregon for a reason. And that's what Roy didn't want to tell me. It was their secret he took to his grave. Anez still probably doesn't know about her mother or she'd have said something. Royal herself might not have known, but probably she did. Anez just thought it was her grandmother's lonely bachelor cousin.
To my girl, Royal.
He was ready, he wanted to try again, write a letter directly to her, his daughter. And it didn't happen. Old Roy. Maybe he died before he could connect in some kind of real way, but he wanted to try.
A four-word story from the pad in his duffel bag. Roy had spent his entire adult life pining for Zena and her daughter, his daughter, Royal. Writing letters for a while to Grandma that didn't look like they were returned, or at least that I could find. What kind of life would that be? My idea of old Roy shifted. I don't exactly know why, but it was different. I'd been thinking of him as a good old guy, like a crusty

beatnik kind of character, going from place to place, hanging out in the woods, looking like Santa Claus. But he was more than that. All his life he thought of them, but never interfered in their lives. Maybe he should have. Maybe that held him back in everything else, because it seemed like he didn't have much at the end. He was ok with it, but maybe because he'd settled. And that's what his whole life was about after Zena and the baby.

But here's another possibility that's kind of fucking sad. He was somebody's dad and they either never knew or just couldn't respond, or something. He knew. Grandma knew. But did *she* know? I could be wrong about all this, I could be off base, but I don't think so.

I'd kept sticky notes, written it out. He'd been up and down the Front Range, to Denver and the suburbs. He was due in the mountains. And he was ahead of the other candidate in the polls, meaning he had the luxury of making campaign stops in out-of-the-way places like this. It was down to just the two of them. The other candidate had said something about a woman's shirt, how nice it looked, especially in two places in front, and women's groups and the media had latched on to it. They'd been about even before, maybe with the other candidate a little ahead.

Georgetown in the morning at the VFW, and then in Frisco in the afternoon, at the old miners' theater. Wasn't sure how to do it. In the pictures in the paper, he'd begun using a cane, and there was Hennie holding his elbow, brushing her hair back, and security. I wanted to reduce the loss of life to just one. The more I thought about it the more the buzz in my head picked up. A headache. A light migraine with a little fluorescent noise, and stiffness. The same feeling I'd had every other time in my life.

My father had told me about his episodes and his Grandfather had told him about his too. All the way back to the Great Grandfather. My blood pressure was way up, and I could hear the sound of my heart beating in my chest. I'd only been sleeping a few hours at night. I couldn't let it go. Dr. Glass had wanted me to talk about it, or write it down, but I couldn't then.

Maybe this is how the bear feels. Once he gets it in his mouth he can't let it go.

Pindar usually spoke for 20 to 30 minutes, and not much Q and A. His car was out front with a driver. His security would be first on the street making a show of it. Then Hennie and finally Pindar. I was across from the theater, upstairs. What I did was check fire escapes in the back and then climb into a vacant building through a window. And it's amazingly easy to buy a high-powered hunting rifle in the mountains. Craigslist.

While I waited I rehearsed my exit. Down the stairs, between the buildings, and in through the side door of the mountaineering shop, or shoppe, and a rented bike waiting. Then here they came. People following him out, talking with their hands going, waving flags and wearing buttons that said *Pindar: The Fire and Rain Campaign*.

Too many people at first and then I saw my moment. The back door of the car had been opened for him and Hennie was walking around. I thought I'd pulled the trigger, thought Pindar was dead, but maybe he'd just stumbled, and maybe the bullet retreated, returned to the rifle, reloaded itself, because in the next second Pindar was in the car and I was sitting on the floor wondering what the hell I was doing, why I was holding a rifle, why I was trying to kill somebody, another somebody.

We were not quite through with the fire season yet. Roger had asked what I was going to do after October, and I said I wasn't sure. He smiled and said I should go and get my I.D. and bring it back. He also offered to let me stay in the cabin for an extra month, and Gail-Emily had already moved out and into an apartment.

But before she left she tried to say something to me.

"Ah, I just wondered," she said, tapping my hands. "Maybe some time we could have a meal, you know, even a Starbucks."

But I didn't know, and Gail-Emily never let me know. I didn't have a clue what she was talking about.

"All right then," she said in this really dramatic, shivery way. "All right. You take care of yourself then, Francis."

You take care, too, I said, and Gail-Emily finished loading her car and drove away.

We had a few more fires to put out before the season was officially over. The last one was above Silverthorne, near the factory outlet stores, in the Eagles Nest Wilderness Area. On the perimeter all of the homeowners were outside with their hoses, giving us instructions for keeping it away from their cabins. These cabins were barely what you'd call rustic though. Except one. And that was the one the fire was headed for.

It was a genuine log cabin with white-painted chinking, with a sleeping porch. And some kind of root cellar-shed. The fire had burned a couple miles the other direction, up to the falls, from a campfire that wasn't put out, and now it was threatening to take the old cabin.

Out of the blue one of the homeowners comes driving up shouting there's a baby inside, there's a baby inside.

Oh, shit, we said, and special-suited up real fast. The thing that made it kind of scary was that they had a big propane tank on the side, near the root cellar. I didn't have a choice but to bash their nice-looking door in and hurry around the place. Lots of old pictures and antique rifles on the walls, but no baby in the rooms. While I'm running around and the fire is bearing down, the homeowner tells the superintendent, "Oh, sorry, I just got a text from my husband and he took the baby, never mind."

When I come out, the supe is really pissed and tells me he thinks there's somebody in the root cellar.

What are they doing with a root cellar up here anyway? I asked.

"No idea," he said, "but we better check to make sure nobody's inside."

I walked to the cellar and kept my eye on the propane. When I got there I booted the door open. Inside was none other than the bear with a broken jar of green beans in his hands, slurping the last of them down.

What the hell are you doing in there? I yelled to the bear.

He said something like Ahhhjeez, ahhhjeez, or that's what it sounded like.

There were tomatoes and okra, pickled beets, and the green beans all over the place.

"Run him out of there," the superintendent shouted. "Make some noise and chase that goddamn bear out of there and get away from there yourself."

I had an angle on it and could see now the fire was turning away from the tank and didn't look like there was major danger. But I could see it was the bear, my friend, the one who'd saved me from the sheriff, and who had bloodied his ear when he ripped the tag out. The one they were looking for.

The supe went back to his truck to get a pistol.

Hey, you gotta leave now, I said. The superintendent's going to come back with a gun and shoot you. No more green beans.

I got a rake and went after the bear. C'mon I said, c'mon. And I hit him with the handle end. He thought I was kidding and broke open another jar of beets, which were that deep red and he sloshed them all over.

The supe took a call but I saw him load a big pistol and stick it in his pocket.

I took the tine-end of the rake and hit the bear as hard as I could. The rake hit him on the face and forehead, on his nose. It stunned him and pissed him off. He came out of the shed in a flash and looked like he might bite me, or rip my face off.

He got close and stopped. The crew moved closer and got their tools ready to knock the shit out of him. With the beet juice all over, he looked ferocious, like he'd already been wounded. And here came the superintendent.

Goddamnit bear, I said hitting him again, and this time he roared, but he also turned away. The crew drew closer but knew enough to leave him an opening, and he took it.

As the bear loped off along the fire line, the supe raised his pistol and popped off a couple shots. When the bear didn't stop the superintendent fired the rest of the rounds, but either he was a bad shot or the bear just ignored him.

I wanted to say goodbye, or hey, see ya, bear, but I felt kind of stupid in front of all the guys, and so I just watched him amble until he'd climbed up over one ridge, then another, and then his black-browness was out of sight. But it seemed like the bear was taking something with him. Something that belonged to him and something that belonged to me.

Ok, then, bear, I said, ok.

17.

Dr. Glass: I'm surprised to see you, Francis. How've you been. And where've you been? As they probably told you up front, this is the last week of the Indigent Program. We weren't refunded.

No, they didn't tell me anything about the program. Sorry to hear about that. I'm just in town to get my I.D. and then I go back up.

Dr. Glass: Where is up, Francis, where are you going back up to? And I notice that you're carrying your notebook, the one I gave you.

Yeah, Dr. Glass, I've taken a few notes, written a few things down.

Dr. Glass: That's great, Francis, I think that could be counted as progress.

I've been working up in the mountains, Dr. Glass, on a crew putting out fires all over the place, but mostly Colorado. I've been on a hand crew but sometimes we did some smoke jumping.

Dr. Glass: That sounds pretty exciting and maybe right down your alley.

You mean because it's dealing with fire and that kinda thing.

Dr. Glass: Oh, no, I meant active-wise, using your size and strength, but maybe fires too.

Well, there is something I like about fire, but I've also had some bad luck with it.

Dr. Glass: Really, like what kind of bad luck?

I almost got burned up myself, and one of my friends, Nils, was killed.

Dr. Glass: I'm sorry to hear that. But you're ok now, aren't you?

A few scars on my legs, and I was afraid to go back for a while.

Dr. Glass: So, Francis, if you don't mind I'd like to change the subject to something very serious. The police have been here and they interviewed me about you and the murder of the officer and the college girl, the basketball player. I had to tell them that without a court order I couldn't talk to them. But they asked me a lot of questions. Tell me about that, Francis. What happened there?

To shorten it up, because there was all this stuff earlier, before the game, we were at the Side Car, a bar on Colfax, after the game and were drinking. The police came, it was after two, and when they saw Poletta . . .

Dr. Glass: This is the girl, the basketball player?

. . . yeah, and when they saw Poletta and that I was driving the Chancellor's car, they let us go and kept everyone else there. They didn't recognize me.

Dr. Glass: How did you come to be driving the Chancellor's car?

He'd hired me to be security, the Twins introduced us, and gave me his car that night after everything was over. The college was in the championship game, and I was supposed to be extra security, he'd had some threats. Poletta was the star of the game and we met up afterward. We drove around town and out on the prairie and then we went to the house.

Dr. Glass: This was the house that was burned down with the two people in it?

Yeah, she wanted to go someplace where we could be together, just the two of us, and I told her about vacant houses, expensive new houses, and that I stayed in them sometimes. She liked that idea and we were having a good time. Poletta was playing music on her phone and dancing. She was taking a shower upstairs when the cop came.

Dr. Glass: Were you going to spend the night there or just hang out for a while?

We had blankets. We were going to stay the night.

Dr. Glass: I think one of the neighbors must have seen some activity. Maybe they thought you were burglars.

We weren't going to do anything, just spend the night.

And then the cop came and he shot Poletta. I tried to warn her, but he saw her and thought she was carrying a gun.

Dr. Glass: Was she carrying a gun? I thought she'd been taking a shower.

She came down to get me, to take a shower with her, and she'd found a caulking gun up there somewhere. She was holding it and maybe the cop thought that was a weapon. She was naked and he shot her twice.

Dr. Glass: Did that upset you a great deal, Francis, when the policeman shot Poletta right in front of you? I imagine that it did. Especially with your headaches.

I was in love with Poletta. Po-Po-letta. She was beautiful and she liked me.

Dr. Glass: What happened with the policeman? How did he get shot? Was there a struggle? Was it an accident?

I struggled with him but he'd already shot Poletta. I couldn't believe it. One minute we were at the basketball game and Poletta was the star. Another minute we were at the bar singing, having a good time. And then we were at the house, listening to music with the lights off, Poletta dancing.

Dr. Glass: Did you shoot the officer, Francis? Did you kill him?

I didn't want Poletta to be dead. I didn't want her blood all over me. I held her. She was the Queen of Hearts, red and black. She was so beautiful. She called me Tall. She was something else.

Dr. Glass: Did you shoot the officer on purpose, Francis? For your sake I want it to be an accident, but I don't think it was, was it?

In the moment when he looked at what he'd done, he looked at Poletta, I knocked the gun out of his hands and hurt him. We struggled but it was over. And I found his gun.

Dr. Glass: You shot him and what about the fire?

I didn't want them to find her in her Queen of Hearts

outfit. I didn't care what happened to the cop, but I didn't want them to find her. So I burned the house down, I did. Then I got away from there.

Dr. Glass: What if you'd caught the neighborhood on fire? What if you'd injured someone else? How would you feel about that?

I was glad to hear no one else was injured. I'd have felt bad if they had been, or even it had touched any of their houses.

Dr. Glass: Francis, I'd like for you to turn yourself in.

I don't think I can do that, Dr. Glass. I'm a different person than I was then. I've changed. Working on the fire crew, out in the woods, has changed me. And I've done a lot of thinking.

Dr. Glass: In a few short months you've changed that much? Doesn't seem possible. I won't say anything to them, but I really would like it if you turned yourself in. I'm willing to call and negotiate for you, help you get an attorney, serve as a reference. How does that sound?

I appreciate the effort, but I can't do that. I'll spend the rest of my life in prison. It's not right, killing that cop, I know, I'm not trying to say it was, and he probably has a family and they miss him, but I was upset that he killed Poletta without waiting, without asking any more questions.

Dr. Glass: If you're not willing to turn yourself in then I'll have to stop these sessions. I don't think I can continue, Francis, I'm sorry.

It's ok, Dr. Glass. You've helped me quite a bit, whether you know it or not. I appreciate it. And I've taken a lot of notes.

Dr. Glass: What will you do now that the fire season is over, now that there's not any work?

They said I could stay in the dorm a little while longer and I'll probably try and get on at one of the ski resorts.

They're about ready to start up. And if I can stay out of trouble I might just see about living in the mountains, starting over there.

Dr. Glass: Good luck to you, Francis, and in the best sense, I hope never to hear from you again. Do you understand my meaning?

I think so, Dr. Glass. Yeah, I think so. Thanks.

18.

Because they didn't run a background check, and because I could start right away, and because they paid pretty well, and because they had housing for the staff, I went to work at the ski resort near Glenwood. This is the dinky place where I was supposed to meet Pindar, the place where they rolled the bomb under the car, and the place where the divot is still there on the road. They put me on lift maintenance, mostly getting the chairs ready, repairing them, reattaching them.

I'd stayed in the Forestry cabin until somebody came and said they needed to close it up.

What happened to four weeks, I said.

"Go talk to Roger," the guy, Randle it said on his shirt, said to me. I'd been reading cowboy novels again, getting up late, walking in the woods, eating cereal every meal. And it was time anyway.

I was still looking over my shoulder whenever I went places like the grocery store or out in public, but nobody said anything.

And here's the deal: Pindar won the election. By a pretty good margin too. And there was Hennie by his side in the pictures. They looked like a couple. And once when I was walking I saw them driving down the street in the *Fire and Rain* limo, this was before he took office, and Hennie saw me and tapped Pindar on the shoulder. He was in the front and she was in the back. They put their windows down and looked at me. The car slowed but it didn't stop. I thought I saw Pindar nod, Hennie too, but maybe not. Maybe I wanted them to nod and say it was over. But they just put the windows of the black car up and drove on.

After I'd started work at the ski resort, I sent Anez a note telling her about the mountains, about the kind of work I was doing, and that if she still had some salmon, I'd like to try it. A week later a box came with a letter.

Hi Francis,

Do you prefer Francis or Fran or Frank? I sent you the smoked pinyon, it's my favorite. The other ones are good, but pinyon is the best. I smoke it for a whole day, overnight actually, low, and I get the wood from someplace outside of Taos. Once I get started I have to keep the fire going for a week, I make a bunch ahead. I sent you a couple pounds. Let me know how you like it.

The picture is of Neza in her step-dancing outfit, she belongs to a group and they go all over the state. We live in Astoria. That's me in the background to the right. Lots of the parents are involved. It's kind of fun and the kids seem to like it.

You asked about Neza's blood problem and it's not really a problem, not like a disease. She has this rare blood type that almost nobody has ever heard of. The only thing is if she ever gets sick or is injured, there's almost nobody around who has her same blood, who could bank it for a transfusion. She inherited it from her dad.

That ski place sounds pretty cool. I had to Google it to see exactly where you were talking about. Send me a picture. I'd like to see you at work.

Sounds like you and Roy became friends there for a while. He might've stayed in shape by working in the woods. Hard to believe he was still doing it at 85. If he was grandma's cousin that makes him my cousin down line, right, like third cousin?

After the ski season and before you go back to work for Forestry, if you're out this way stop in. I got the job, incidentally, but I have to run now and I'll tell you about it later.

Anez

The ski season was about to get started. Maybe a week or ten days away. Wet storms were building off the Mexican and California coasts. The bigger resorts were already making snow for their bases. We had almost all the equipment up and running, with just a few things left to fix. I was learning a lot about maintaining a ski resort in short order.

In the dorm it wasn't the same as being with old Roy or the others, but it was all right. Everybody had computers and they were on the internet from the second they got home. And some of them just used their phones. The resort gave me a leftover cell. We had like a little cafeteria that served the basics and that's where all of us ate when we didn't go into town.

"How do you get around with no car?" the guys asked.

I manage, I said, and told them I had a truck in Denver. I didn't say it was a truck that belonged to the new governor, that I stole from his ranch. This group didn't call me Tallman or Big Boy, though they brought it up, but they liked to refer to me as The Old Guy. Most of them were in their early twenties and I'm 29, so they thought of me as the old guy on the mountain. Figure that.

Anez's smoked salmon came in a box but it was hard to disguise the smell. I bought saltines and shared the fish with everyone. It was great stuff and I sent her a letter and a picture with all of us feasting on it and one of me on a lift tower. There was six in our bunch and eight in the cabin across from us. The salmon lasted one night when the other group heard about it.

I wanted to say something to Anez about my discovery, about Royal, but thought I'd wait till she gave me a little clue that it would be ok to bring it up. Maybe she figured it out, maybe her mother knew, so maybe I was making too big of a deal over it.

A day before the first storm, Anez's short letter came.

Francis,

Thanks for the pix. Glad everybody liked the salmon.

The job is with the Portland Jewish Federation's senior apartment complex. I work three six-hour shifts. I like it already and they like me, which is a good thing. Because I had to leave early once for Neza and come in late.

Hey, and even my mom thinks you look a little like Neza's dad. That's a good thing.

Anez

All the resorts got a big dumping, including ours, and it was good to finally get people on the slopes. Mostly families, kids, a few snowboarders. This is not a real challenging hill, one black run, but it's not all that easy either. I never thought I'd like skiing, never saw myself as the skier type, but every day I've been trying it out, and I'm starting to get the hang of it.

And re the work, a couple of days we had to do twenty-four, with eight off, and then back on again, which was real hard, especially with a kid boss, but I kept my mouth shut and the kid bought me a beer later and told me how he appreciated my help. Skiing is one of those things that started off as a bad deal, oh, shit, it's snowing, and now they're charging people up the ass for putting high-tech barrel slats on their feet and dragging them up the hill in a plastic bubble.

I sent Anez another note asking for more salmon and included money to pay for it. I circled around a little bit, talked about how the season was going, and then finally said something about old Roy's medals and badges, he had a collection of them, like a dozen or so, and didn't she think it was interesting how their names were similar, her mother's name and Roy's name, and wondered if that name was common in their family. I included a picture of me in skis on the slope.

Because I was starting to get interested in Anez, what I knew about her, I didn't want to come right out and say something about Neza's dad, so I tried asking whether he was working and between the two of them were they still having a hard time making ends meet?

Seemed like Anez barely had time to open my letter and think about it. Right away it was there in the mail at the main office.

After the intro, in the first line, she said,

*I've wondered about that a couple times myself, Francis.
Roy and Royal. Maybe Grandma Zena just liked Roy's
name, she was kind of a cowgirl and it has a cowboy
sound, or she did it to remember her first boyfriend, or
it was just one of those things, hard to say. I'll ask my
mom. Can't think of any other people with that name
in our family, though.*

*And about Neza's dad, he always lived on the danger-
ous side, he was an iron worker, and he was up on one
of the bridges they were putting across the Columbia.
He wasn't strapped in and fell. He lasted a few days
but didn't survive. We were doing ok between the two
of us, and there was insurance money after, but it ran
out. Neza was just a year old, she doesn't remember him
much. My mom helped us and basically gave us this
house, but we still struggle.*

How about you?

Anez

Yeah, how about me? What to say and what to write? The
truth? I've been in trouble, Anez. I burned up an old west
town. I've actually killed some people. The governor tried to
blow me up. My family is strange, my blood is strange too,
like Neza's, and we're descended from. . . .
 I'll make some things up. I'm a college guy. I've been an
entrepreneur. I have a nice car.

Anez,
I said something chitty-chatty about eating way too much

190

pizza and that I was reading another Western about a white man raised by Apaches who saves people in a stagecoach.

Are you a reader, Anez? I asked.

I like Westerns.

I'm starting to enjoy this little place and the people. Learning to really like the outdoors, too. One of the things I've noticed is the hawks floating around while we're working. Lots of red-tails and we've spotted an eagle's nest up high by a run.

This is a little bit cheaper resort, so we get more families who can't afford the bigger places like Breck, or even Aspen. Nobody can afford that place anymore except professional athletes and Brad Pitt.

For a while I lived in Denver, then I was out on a ranch east of town, in Doveless. I grew up all around, but mostly Colorado. I've got a sister somewhere, a half-brother I haven't heard from. Both my parents are dead.

I miss old Roy and his tomato soup. And I miss the bear.

I thought I'd let her ask me what I meant by "I miss the bear." Which made me wonder where he was. They never said if they saw him or shot at him or found his trail. Seems like we'd know if they dragged him out. He's out there right now wondering what the hell to do with himself, where he can find another jar of green beans, and where to find a nice place to snooze for a few months.

There was a little more blah-blah, and then I signed off.

But I waited for that whole week and the next. No letter. Three weeks, and then finally one came.

Hi Francis,

Didn't know Roy was such a cook. But didn't know that much about him anyway. Was it canned tomato with something in it or a recipe he completely made up. I have one I make with garlic and a little salmon, fresh heirlooms, and basil. It's the best ever. Nezi likes it because I make her favorite grilled cheese with it. But she doesn't eat much of the soup with the fish in it.

No idea what "missing the bear" meant. Was that a bear that came around, or a pet bear. Probably a lot of them up there. Maybe even some are skiers. LOL

And my mom. Your question or observation didn't seem like that big of a deal. But when I said something about Roy and Royal, how similar they were, she went outside and stood on the back porch.

I asked her what was up and you'll never guess what she said.

So, guess, I'm listening.

Anez

Three different ways, that's how many times it took before I got the letter started and written. I didn't have to guess what she said. I was right. Her mother, Royal, knew and had been keeping it to herself, for whatever reason. She and Grandma Zena, probably Grandpa too, all three knew, and those two dead now. But after I'd had a few days to think about it, I had a bunch of questions: Why didn't they do anything about it?

192

Why not invite the old guy around, come out for a visit, they could've said, meet your daughter, hi Dad, that sort of thing? Old Roy, good-hearted Roy, harmless Roy, a little-bit-fucked-up Roy, lonely-ass Roy, dead Roy.

He was Royal's dad and she never acknowledged him, or so it seemed. Whatever the reason, it doesn't sound right from here. Maybe I don't know all the details, or Roy said or did something early on, or maybe he should've tried harder to make contact himself, or maybe Zena's family-rejection thing continued on, or Grandma and Grandpa just decided better to let sleeping dogs lie, or some such thing, and Royal went with that. None of it sounds worth a damn, whatever happened.

I didn't want to talk to Anez for a while, after I got to rumbling around about it. I didn't ever want to meet her mother for sure. And I was just going to hold on to his stuff for the time being, instead of packing it up and shipping it, some of it, which is what I'd planned to do. Fuck those people. And I just folded up the great letter I'd written and stuck it in my back pocket.

A second letter came after five weeks, though.

All it said on a little pink sticky was "Are you still guessing?"

No, I said to myself, I'm not still guessing. I just wanted a little justice for Roy, that's all. But I had to laugh at Ancz. Persistent.

New letter.

Anez,

Sorry, I haven't written. But, actually, I'm not still guessing. I knew the answer in the first place. Roy was your mom's real dad, right? And maybe people didn't

193

ever want to talk about it. And old Roy never pushed it. And one day led to the next, people meant to talk, but they just never got it done. And now your grandparents are gone and Roy's passed too. It's more than unfortunate for your mother. She never got to know Roy, and in just the few weeks I'd gotten to know him, I thought he was a pretty good guy, a unique old soul.

Did your mother give you the whole story? Pass it along if you feel comfortable and your mother's ok with it.

I'd use the internet except I'm not that good at it. I've learned to ski, though, and if I can do that, I can probably learn to use the internet.

Francis

Francis,

Did Roy say something to you? I wonder how you knew? There were probably a few clues you put together, right, from hanging out with him and maybe from the stuff he left. I said something to my mother and she broke down crying. I don't know how I missed a thing like that. Roy was her father, and my grandfather, not my cousin.

At first my mother didn't want to talk about it. Even though she's older it's still a sensitive issue, I guess. Why didn't we ever meet Roy? I asked. Did you ever invite him out for a visit? Why didn't we send him cards, Christmas presents? Did he ever marry and have another family? Shouldn't we have tried to call him, find him?

My mother said it wasn't quite like that; in fact, it wasn't like that at all. And that she used to talk with Roy on the phone when she was a little girl, they wrote each other letters, he sent her money, and they had plans to meet every summer. But then she got busy and sometimes maybe even missed her phone appointments. "I was being a girl," she told me while she was crying. They kept planning to do things. But then she turned 13 and became a teenager. She sent him a picture. People said she looked a lot like Grandma Zena at that age. They talked once, after a long time of missing, and she told him she was having trouble with Grandma and wanted to get on the bus and go to Colorado to live, finish high school there. After that he never talked with her again, they never talked. Not by phone. Not by letter. Nothing.

They thought that maybe he'd died suddenly or gotten sick. They tried to contact him in every way they could, including through the unfriendly uncles and aunts in Denver. Nobody could find him.

I thought I knew everything about my mother. After all these years.

What do you think about this, Francis, as a non-family member?

How's the ski training coming? Is the dorm warm? Is it all guys?

Bye for now.

Anez

Before I gave Roy's belongings away I looked all through them, pockets and things, inside out, starting with his shoes. I thought he might have hidden one of Royal's letters somewhere, but no. I'd looked before but this time I did it more carefully. It's interesting to find out things about another human being, but by going through and looking at their personal belongings, but when they're dead. Take Roy's shoes, for instance. They were one of the expensive brands and were made in Montana. I wouldn't have expected it from him. They were nice shoes, black, and good leather, but a plain style with a capped toe. When I lifted the tongue, I could see his footprint in the shoe, and where the ball pressed down and his toes, especially his big toe, leaned into the leather. These were clearly shoes he'd had a long time and he took care of them. On both of the heels he had rubber taps stuck onto the back corners and they'd been replaced more than once, there were leftover tacks.

At the bottom of the legs of his pants, you could see that they were too long, or his legs were too short, and that they were frayed, right where they dragged or touched the ground a little, above the tap. I remember Roy had the habit of kind of slapping the top of his thighs, grinding his hands a little, to emphasize a point, and right there the jeans were extra worn. He had a brown belt in his bag and it had plenty of oil stains on it, from his hands and fingers, and it was way too long. He used the sixth hole on the belt and it had been poked wide open and made dark. He was a skinny-assed runt of a guy.

One of the plaid flannel shirts I'd given away had worn spots on the elbows, I noticed, and every time I saw Roy wearing it he had the sleeves rolled up. He did it for style, but also because he bought his shirts too big, maybe to compensate for being small.

In the bag there was his wool stocking cap rolled up,

gloves, white socks with worn heels, no black or colored ones, and big white underwear, with dribbled stains in the front. I think Roy had that disease old men get where they take a piss and their dicks continue to leak, or they leak trying to get to the bathroom. He spent a lot of time going back and forth to the outhouse.

After I got everything out and had laid it on the bed, I got to thinking that this bag full of stuff represented a guy's life, Roy's life, the standing-up, walking-around part of his life, the what-people-could-see part of who he was. And just sifting through it, I got another hit about him, more than what I already knew. Even though he was a woodsy, Beatnik kind of character, with a little bit of gayness, he had a traditional side, a plain-black-shoes side, a white-socks-and-plain-white-underwear side.

For the wool shirt that was laying in front of me, I'd checked the left breast pocket once before and there was a couple of hidden sunflower seeds at the bottom when I checked it this time. But I spaced out looking in the right side somehow. Both the buttons on either side were knocked off the pockets, and the collar was worn through to the liner, especially in the back. When I reached inside the right this time, though, there was a little beat-up rectangle of paper, a two-by-three, with writing on the back, and taped over numerous times.

Hi Roy, it said in the fancy but faded pen of a teenaged girl, *this was taken at the Sno-Ball. I'm wearing my. . . .* It was all hard to read and the end part had disappeared completely.

On the front was a fresh-looking girl, grinning with nice teeth, wearing a white uniform and gold chain around her neck, maybe a football dangling from it. It was a picture of Royal in some kind of cheering outfit with a note to her father on the back.

Roy's thin brown wallet was in the bag, too, another

thing I never saw before, but it was stuck in a hidden flap on the side. There was nothing in the wallet to speak of, no money, no receipts, except a driver's license and an ancient SSI card, with markings along the top and sides for the monthly amounts he'd been receiving - $635, $790, $844, $976, and $1108. He was still working even though he got Social Security.

And my guess, something I've been doing more of lately, is that the photo with the message on the back was probably one of the last real communications Roy and Royal ever had. Royal tried to make contact after that, sounds like, some kind, repeatedly, but it didn't happen, or two-way anyway. Roy didn't let it.

Anez's note came today. And I knew before I opened it what it was about, part of it anyway.

Francis,

How's the skiing? I've never actually had skis on, it's always seemed so dangerous, and expensive, and I'm such a klutz. There are places around here, you can see them from the highway, but that's as close as I've gotten.

So, here's my question: Why do you suppose Roy never wrote back or contacted my mother when she said she wanted to move out there with him, knowing what you know? It hurt her feelings a lot, I talked with her for a while about it, made her really worried, too, and took her a long time to get over it. She felt totally rejected, and after that she thought about him quite a bit, and then as she got older and nothing happened she just kind of gave up thinking about having any kind of relationship.

By the way, you said something in one of your letters about having a blood condition, too, maybe like Neza's, and I wondered what it was. When I told Neza, she was pretty curious. There are so few with her type around here, or anywhere.

Alright then. Think about stopping out after ski season. I'll show you how I smoke the fish.

Bye,

Anez

I had it wrong. Roy was getting ready to write Royal a note, but it wasn't because they had ignored him. It was the other way around. After a lifetime, he finally thought he'd reach out to her again. They'd had a relationship when she was a girl, then it got a little sketchy, and finally, when Royal became a teenager and wanted to come out to visit, Roy got really cold feet and quit it all together. And I have an idea about why he did that. The deep background, as Dr. Glass would say.

Two parts: One, Royal looked too much like Grandma Zena and Roy didn't know what to do about that. He probably got to reminiscing, looking at the picture, thinking about them so many years ago, his one and only girlfriend. And two, Royal coming represented starting up a relationship, a whole ball of wax he didn't know if he could handle. A thirteen-year-old girl, even though it was his own daughter, living with him in his Beatnik world. He'd had his heart broken by Grandma once before, and he'd gone a good part of his life without any more of that kind of pain, so he was pretty sure he didn't want to do it again. But why not give something else a try? Short visits here or out there? Internet talking. Letters with plenty of pictures. Long phone calls. A vacation meet-up. Who knows. But Roy going his whole life without meeting his daughter, when he could've, seems like, I don't know, one of those really bad deals for both parties. But we know she'd been thinking about it. And Roy was probably carrying around a lot more than her taped up picture in his right pocket.

His four-word story: *To my girl, Royal.*

As the season got closer to the end, they asked me if I'd stick around a little extra, help them get the place shut down. My boss, the kid, asked me a couple times where he knew me from, he felt like he knew me from somewhere, and I told him maybe in Denver, that I'd worked all over. I actually had a real good idea, and as a wise guy thought of saying Did this have anything to do with killing a cop or burning down an old west town with the security guard inside? But that's the kind of statement that would land me back in trouble.

In the notebook Dr. Glass had given me, I'd begun to scribble words and things, even a few drawings, I might want to say to her in a letter. But I wasn't quite sure what I wanted to talk about. Or what I should even bring up. Except that I'd been having the nightmares again.

I really regret. . . .

I could hear her asking "What is it that you regret, Francis?"

Dr. Glass:

I've wanted to talk to you in person, and I know that's not possible now, so I thought I'd write a letter. Hope you don't mind. And I understand that you probably won't be able to respond.

There was more than one.

You asked me a few times.

I just thought I'd start with a clean plate.

The guy at the parking lot.

The security guard at the old west town.

The cop in the house who shot Poletta.

Terp.

Almost Pindar.

And one a long time ago nobody knows about.

I regret what happened with all of them, killing them, I do. And none of the excuses—what they might've said or done to provoke me—are any good.

My grandfather killed someone once, my father, too, I watched them both do it. It has been in our blood for a long time–at least since Doctor created Great Grandfather. And it seemed like my Father and Grandfather doing that gave me permission. Each time I've had regrets, though, bad regrets, migraines, dreams, which we've talked about, but it was wrong to do what I did, no getting around it.

Fighting fires and working at the resort have helped me change, being outdoors will do that. I was looking for a way to shift anyway, but they gave me the time and opportunity. Almost getting burned up myself did something too. And being there when Nils died made me think about life a lot more. His, mine, and other people's.

I can do it different, Dr. Glass, I know you don't think so, but I can. Might tumble down the slope a few times, not on the killing people part, in general, but I'll get back up, struggle with it some more.

Can the Francis Stein story change, make a detour? The answer is a hardcore We'll see.

Francis

Coda

I said before I didn't ever want to talk to Anez's mother, Royal, after the way I thought she treated old Roy, but when I found out what happened to her, to Roy, even to Grandma Zena, who suffered in her own way, I had to back off. And how about this: Royal sent me a letter, with a picture of the three of them, inside one of Anez's.

She asked me a few questions about Roy, what I thought he died of, if he was healthy before that, where it happened, why he was still working in the woods, and where he was buried.

I told her everything I could figure out, about him dying of a heart attack, my guess, that he seemed pretty healthy and didn't act like he had heart problems or that he took any meds, that it happened in the kitchen of a Forestry cabin in the woods south of Lake Dillon, that I thought he just liked working outdoors, and that I buried him myself where I figured he wanted to be buried—outside near a stream.

Maybe one day when Anez and I come to visit you can show me his grave, Royal said in her next note. Anez and I swapped a few more letters and they sent me a picture of Grandma Zena, Roy's heartthrob. I studied the photo and didn't say anything back about it. She was wearing overalls and straddling a big red horse and was more of a handsome woman than really pretty. I thought about Roy and Grandma Zena, Roy and Grandma Zena, and came away with an observation: they weren't a match. Sorry old Roy wherever you are. I could just see in her eyes and face, the way she held herself, she was a smart, spunky kind of woman and eventually there would've been a problem, a split-up. Even though they were sweet on each other as kids, the parents were right to send her away to Oregon. My two cents, but I think I'm right. Still, too bad about old Roy and Royal.

He said something to me once when we were sitting outside at the cabin. He made a statement after he'd smoked some weed about never measuring up, that he thought if he could just show her, Zena, what a good worker and money maker he was that maybe she would like him, want to be with him. He was still thinking this way at 85. Then he changed the subject because it looked like his eyes had filled with tears.

The ski resort had a van they didn't need and I bought it from them for a thousand bucks. Had some scrapes on both sides and the back, and it was plain white, stick, with the resort's name still on it, but the mechanic said it was in good shape.

I thought I would take in the Tetons, spend a couple nights in Idaho, then push on into Oregon. I told Anez I was thinking about heading that direction and she gave me her phone, said she had plenty of rooms.

I got up on 80 from Glenwood and turned north on 191 at Rock Springs. It was a good day, actually, the sun was out, but still cool, and the road was dry. There was lots of good antelope country all around on the way to Jackson's Hole, the town by the Tetons.

Coming out of a roadside rest from taking a piss, I saw

somebody I recognized trying to hitch a ride. This was one of the people from the Christian breakfast in Denver. I pulled over and he was shivering, could barely talk. He said he'd been standing there all night and it had gotten damn cold. I turned on the heater full blast and we talked about Denver, as best he could.

When I asked where he was headed he said, "The Tetons, man, I was gonna stop at one of those fuckin' campgrounds and rob somebody, get their vehicle and their parka, fuck 'em up. You in for some of that action?"

I looked at Peckham carefully, that's what his name was, and saw myself on the passenger's side, sitting exactly where he was sitting. Peckham didn't have a hat and was wearing a short-sleeved shirt. His hair was wild looking and dirty and he smelled like he'd been next to a campfire. I don't think I ever looked as bad as that, but he reminded me of my time driving on the lake and after.

Peckham, I said, how the hell did you get here?

He thought I meant how did he get to the physical place he was at on the side of the road.

"Took me about ten rides, man," he said, "used to be I could do it in one or two."

I wondered what brought him to this spot, this time in his life, and what his plan was, aside from fucking campers up. I couldn't tell how old he was. One second his face looked like he was 25 and the next 55.

"What you been up to, Tallman?" he asked, looking me over. Had I been a foot shorter he'd have beaten me up, taken the van.

Peckham, I said shaking my head, reach back there and get that wool blanket and that stocking cap.

He hadn't stopped shivering yet.

"Thanks, man. You're looking kind of professional, kind of successful with that nice jacket. You been working up here?"

I told him about the resort, working on the chairlift, and learning to ski.

He wanted to know where I was headed and I told him Oregon, and he said that's where he was going.

"What part?" he asked.

I pulled over and said I thought I could feel a problem with the rear passenger tire, could he check to see if it was low. He got out and walked back to look. In the side mirror, I could see him adjusting the wool blanket around his shoulders and kicking the tire.

In what seemed like an incredibly lengthy moment, I reached over and pulled the passenger door shut, shifted the van into gear, and drove away.

"Hey, goddamnit, hey," I could hear him yelling.

In the rearview I stared at him for a long time as I drove down the highway.

Peckham, sorry, I said out loud, I didn't have any choice, man, we'd never have made it to Oregon. I just couldn't take you with me, couldn't have you around.

And Peckham, I said, more than leaving you behind, I had to leave myself behind.

When I got far enough away, I looked at the map and retraced where I was, where I was going to be stopping, and how far away Astoria was.

At the Oregon state line, I'd call Anez so it wasn't too big of a surprise, or problem, and let her know.

The Rh Blood Group System

The Rh blood group system consists of at least 45 independent antigens and was first described in 1939. It is one of the most polymorphic and immunogenic systems and, next to ABO, is the most clinically significant blood groups in transfusion medicine.

Rhnull Phenotype

Rhnull phenotype (also referred to as Rhnull syndrome or Rhnull disease) is a rare blood group with a reported frequency of approximately 1 in 6 million individuals. The characteristic hallmark of Rhnull phenotype is the lack of all Rh antigens on the RBCs. In addition to lacking Rh antigens, Rhnull cells also lack LW and Fy5, and have a reduced expression of Ss, U, and Duclos antigens.

Rhnull and Antibodies

In Rhnull subjects the commonest antibody formed in response to transfusion or pregnancy reacts with all cells except Rhnull cells.

Rhnull Genetic Mechanisms

The Rhnull is produced by at least two different genetic mechanisms. The 'amorph' type is the result of molecular change in RHCE gene with a deleted RHD gene, whereas the more common 'regulator' type is associated with the defect in RHAG gene. Both genotypes result in the same clinical syndrome characterised by chronic haemolysis of varying severity, with stomatocytosis, spherocytosis, increased osmotic fragility, altered phospholipids asymmetry, altered cell volume, defective cation fluxes, and elevated Na+/K+ ATPase activity.

About the Author

A. Rooney is an associate professor who teaches writing at Jindal Global University in Sonipat, India when not in Denver. He has published a collection of stories, *The Colorado Motet* (Ghost Road Press) and a novella, *Fall of the Rock Dove* (Main Street Rag). His stories and poems have appeared in journals, magazines and websites all over the world.